THE YACHT PEOPLE

Borgo Press Books by Michael Hemmingson

The Rose of Heaven
In the Background Is a Walled City
How to Have an Affair and Other Instructions
Barry N. Malzberg: Beyond Science Fiction
Auto/Ethnographies: Sex, Death, and Independent Filmmaking
Sexy Strumpets and Troublesome Trollops
Seven Women
Hold Me, Please, and Say This Is Love
Give Me the Gun, She Says
Judas Payne

FOR OTHER PRESSES

The Naughty Yard (Permeable Press, 1994)
Crack Hotel (Permeable Press, 1995)
Minstrels (Permeable Press, 1997)
The Mammoth Book of Short Erotic Novels (Carroll & Graf, 2000)
The Mammoth Book of Legal Thrillers (Carroll & Graf, 2001)
Wild Turkey (Forge, 2001)
The Comfort of Women (Blue Moon, 2002)
The Dress (Blue Moon, 2002)
My Fling with Betty Page (Eraserhead Press, 2003)
Drama (Blue Moon, 2003)
The Rooms (Blue Moon, 2003)
The Lawyer (Blue Moon, 2003)
House of Dreams Trilogy (Avalon, 2004)
The Garden of Love (Blue Moon, 2004)
Expelled from Eden: A William T. Vollmann Reader (Thunder's
    Mouth Press, 2004)
Short & Sweet (Blue Moon, 2006)
William T. Vollmann: Freedom, Redemption, and Prostitution
    (McFarland, 2008)
Star Trek: TV Milestone (Wayne State Univ. Press, 2009)
*Gordon Lish and His Influence on 20th Century Literature: The Life
    and Times of Captain Fiction* (Routledge, 2009).
The Reflexive Gaze of Critifiction (Guide Dog Books, 2009)

THE YACHT PEOPLE

AN EROTIC PRIVATE EYE YARN

by

MICHAEL HEMMINGSON

The Borgo Press
An Imprint of Wildside Press LLC

MMIX

www.wildsidepress.com

FIRST EDITION

DEDICATION

This one has to be for

Dominique Navarro

for instigating this book
with her neurosis and anger

&

is a *homage* to those great, forgotten old
perverted private eye novels written by

Carter Brown

PART I

I went in search of myself.
                    —HERACLITUS

CHAPTER ONE

She didn't tell me that she was a *squirter*.

It's not the sort of thing an apparent one-night stand lets loose after a few drinks, some making out, the pulling off of the clothes and the inevitable, eventual screw. I guess I can say it was a pleasant surprise, like the way a plumber grins when a pipe he's working on suddenly bursts and sprays all over him.[*]

There we were, in my sailboat—a 30-foot Catalina—awkwardly squeezed onto my cabin bed; we were both half naked and her legs were spread and I was going down on her. I was having a fairly fun time eating her out, and then she shook and grunted and filled my mouth with her thick and tangy ejaculate.

There was a lot.

---

[*] I once knew a woman who had a fetish for plumbers, but that's a story to tell on another day.

I mean *a lot.*

"Wow," I said, pulling back and spitting some of that wild stuff out.

"Sorry," she said rather seriously, grabbing at my hair like it was horse reigns; "sometimes I get *carried away* when I get so excited and carried away."

Again, I said, "Wow," with the wonder of a bright-eyed teenage football hero after his first blowjob from a randy and dandy cheerleader during the eve of senior year.

She asked: "Do you mind?"

"No; I like it."

"I *bet* you do," she said, "slut."

"Hm?"

"You heard me."

I was amused, to say the least, of the situation. "Lady, did you just call me a 'slut'?"

"I *know* what you are," she said, "and my name is Erin. I'm *hardly* a lady, not in *this* position."

Erin, yes, Erin—I think she may have even told me that when I met her in the Yacht Club, adjacent to the Marriott Marina Hotel in downtown San Diego; you didn't have to live on one of the hundreds of boats docked at there to wine and dine and dance and mingle in the Yacht Club, although many of the people around, at any given time of the day, did own and live on a boat. I had seen her there at the bar before, or maybe she's the one who spotted me. We'd crossed paths once or twice.

She sat down next to me and asked my name and asked if I'd buy her a drink. "If you tell me yours," I said, being as coy as I could at the moment.

She misheard me. "If I *show* you mine? I need to have at least three strong drinks in my sexy flat stomach before I show it to you, buddy."

Actually, it was more like six, but who counts these days?

And there we were on my little boat—she showed me hers, I did my thing, she turned on the water-works...and then I showed her what *I* had.

Her eyes brightened and she wiggled her nose like the witch on *Bewitched*.

"I always wanted to suck on a private dick," she said, reaching down and taking me in her mouth. She knew what she was doing, that's for sure, that's all that needs to be said; she'd been blowing cock since the beginning of time, since the Big Bang, for billions of years—*she was that good.*

"Play with my balls," I told her.

"Umm."

"Suck those nuts."

"Umm."

"Eat my crotch..."

She did, with her long shiny fingernails running over my skin...

* * * * * * *

"Are you really a gumshoe?" she asked after I came in her mouth.

I was feeling pretty relaxed at the moment. I said, "Where did you hear that?"

"Gossip around the docks."

"Oh?"

"People talk."

"They always do, don't they?" I had to smile. "The *fuckers*; the talking fuckers."

Her voice was low: "I'm sure you've heard plenty of *bad* things about me."

"Not at all," I said. I zipped my trousers up. "I've just found out for myself just how juicy you can be."

She gave me this look, it was like ha-ha: I guess she didn't find my comment on her pussy flow amusing.

"No need to pout," I said.

"No need to be so *crude,*" she said. "So is it true? You're a private detective?"

"Was."

"You were fired? Lost your license?"

"Retired."

"You don't look older than forty."

"Thanks. Gee."

"I mean it."

"I'm thirty-five."

"Nice," she said.

"I don't do that work anymore," I said.

"Why not?"

"I'd rather sit around on my boat," I said.

"Sounds boring," she said.

"It has its moments," I said.

"You don't have any other goals in life?" she asked.

"Except for drinking and getting picked up by women I barely know in bars," I said, "no, not really."

"Are you insinuating I initiated this?" she said.

I raised a curious brow, like Mr. Spock in *Star Trek.*

"You cocky bastard," she said, reaching over to hit me on the arm.

I shrugged.

We stood there and looked at each other and it was a stupid moment.

"You don't know shit about *shit*," she said, and quickly left me alone on my boat.

* * * * * * *

My boat. I never saw myself as a boat person, and then one day I obtained some incriminating evidence on a client's estranged wife, saving him a bundle of cash and a headache on the divorce settlement. Along with a hefty bonus, he said, "How would you like a boat? It's not a yacht or anything, but it's cozy and could be fun and I don't need it; I'd like you to have it." I said why not and figured I could always sell it. The boat sat in the marina docks, under my name, the mooring fee coming out of my checking count each month, for nearly three years. I let friends from out of town or having domestic problems stay on it now and then, but for the most part it sat there on the waterfront: empty. Every month I kept telling myself to put an ad in the paper and get rid of it but always seemed to forget; perhaps subconsciously I didn't want to get rid of it. Which, it seems, was a good thing. My life was quiet and uneventful until that night I fucked Erin. I was no longer interested in excitement, adventure, sordidness and crime after I took three .38 slugs in the gut during a really stupid case, was in the hospital for three months, was told over and over, "It's a miracle you're still alive." So I quit the private eye biz and moved onto this boat, living on savings and taking my time deciding on what the next career would be…let's face it: I wasn't cut out to be a P.I. any-more—or a hit man.

----

* * * * * *

The stupid case. I remember thinking: Looked like it was going to rain, the way the clouds were gathering. Down-town San Diego was packed with all sorts of Saturday night party people. I was wearing a long leather trench; my hair was greasy and messy and I knew I had dark circles under my eyes. I couldn't sleep, because what I was about to do, something I didn't do as a shamus: kill people for money. But the people I was going to kill deserved it.

I went to one of the topless bars near the harbor. The doorman checked my ID, gave me a glance, said: "Something eating you, buddy?"

"Eh?"

"Seem a little nervous there. Never been to a titty and pussy club?"

Grinned. Lied: "Well, I just got out of the pen."

He nodded. "Enjoy."

There were two stages, two girls; the girls changed every third song. When they didn't dance, they served drinks. I ordered a pitcher of beer but I didn't drink.

I watched the backroom.

I saw a fat man in a good suit come out, count some bills from the register and then go back in.

Got up and followed him.

Didn't knock on the office door that had a little sign: PRIVATE.

Underneath the trench, I retrieved the sawed-off pump-action I'd been toting, hiding, waiting—yes—nervously to use, for this very moment.

Barged in.

All three of them were fat and their shirts were dirty, stained from fallen food; but their suits were real nice and they had shit-eating grins as they counted the money in front of them.

"Hey," one of them started to say, "you're—"

Then he saw the sawed-off.

Another one went for the .38 revolver tucked in his stretched waistline.

"Tsk, tsk," I went, and waved the sawed-off.

The third went for the phone.

"Nope," I said.

"Hey, asshole," the fat fuck who got the money from the register said, "what the hell do you want, bub?"

"Ah, the Martoni brothers," I said. "Best pizza this side of town. Best sleazy stripper joint, too."

"Yeah, that's us," said one of the brothers. "Who are you?"

"A dancer used to work here."

"Lots of dancers work here. They comes and goes."

"Her name was Rhonda Littlefield."

Silence.

"You know what I'm talking about. She was murdered three months ago."

One of them said: "Yeah, poor Rhonda."

Another said: "What about her?"

A third said: "We had nothing to do with that."

I said: "She was my sister."

"She hung around the wrong kind of people, you know?" I was told. "Her own fault."

The door behind me opened. I opened started shooting. One of the dancers came in—fake platinum blonde with fake tits, wearing a bra and a g-string. She started to say something and stopped when she saw me and the sawed-off.

"Get in," I said and grabbed her thin arm.

"Is this a hold-up?" she said, chewing bubble gum.

I pushed her toward the Martoni brothers and said, "Just stay put and keep quiet."

"You want money, is that it?" one of the brothers asked me. "Here it is, pal, take it."

"What I want," I said, "is to know which one of you fat fucks killed my sister."

Silence.

"Hey, you knew Rhonda L., right?" one of them asked the platinum blonde.

She had to think about it. "Rhonda? Yeah, sure. We hung out once or twice."

"Well, this is her brother, that's what he says. You tell him how she was. Picking up strange men from this place all the time. Never safe. Drugs. She just got with one of the weirdoes, cut her up and stuff. We had nothing to do—you tell him, Lynn, you tell the brother what kind of nasty bitch his sister was."

The platinum blonde was shaking now. She looked at the sawed-off, then me, said, "Rhonda L. was kind of wild, you know."

"I know one of you did it," I said. "All I want—which one? Which one?—or I blow all three of you whales away."

One of them said, "Hey, boy, where do you get such an idea it was one of us? We're not like that."

With my free hand, I took out a small diary from the trench pocket. "Chronicles of a life, penned by Rhonda Littlefield," I said. "Talks all about how she goes to work at one of the Martoni Brothers Pizza Houses. Then she gets talked into working here: wiggling tits and ass, flashing her cunt and serving drinks. Tells all about how she gets coaxed into bed by one of the Martoni brothers—no name, just one of them. 'They're all fat and disgusting,' she writes. But she goes to bed with this fat fucker because he knows about her secret—a little habit-now-problem with cocaine. So he gets her hooked on more so she'll sleep with him. Then, one day, she winds up dead in a cheap motel room. Now, I either find out which one of you killed her, or you all die."

Silence.

Two of them turned and looked at the third brother.

The third one said: "Okay, I gave her blow and she…was friendly. But I didn't kill her, pal. She liked to play rough, with me, with anyone. I didn't kill her."

I shot his head off.

It was messy.

The two remaining brothers had their dead brother's blood, bone and brain all over them.

The platinum blonde held a hand over her mouth.

Then I took out the other two the same way.

The blonde and I stared at each other.

The music in the club was loud; no one heard the shot-gun fire.

"Are you going to kill me too?" she asked very softly.

"You never saw my face," I said. "You never saw me at all."

"Never! Never! I don't know what you look like, I didn't even know there was someone in here with—"

"That's good."

"Oh man what a mess," she said. "Can I scream now? I really need to."

"When I'm gone."

"How will I—"

"Three minutes," I said, and started to go.

"Hey, you really Rhonda L.'s brother?"

I tossed her the diary and she caught it nervously. "Keep it. Write in it."

Her mouth opened and the bubble gum fell out when she saw that all the pages were blank.

"How did," she started to say, "how…?"

I turned to leave.

It should have been the end of that, end of the story. But:

"Hey, asshole."

I stopped and turned around. She had the .38 one of the fat brothers tried to go for. She pointed it at me and shot three times.

I was in shock. I walked away.

I walked down the street, bleeding. I was dizzy. The first payphone I saw, I called 911.

CHAPTER TWO

"Hey there, Hollywood Square."

I was sitting in the Yacht Club on my second vodka tonic when Erin and a robust fellow in his 50s with a bald head, a great tan, a white beard and a white sports coat with blue slacks sat down across from me.

"Erin," I said.

"I'd like you to my husband, Bobby," she said.

The man shook my hand and his grip was tight but there didn't seem to be any anger in either his grip or eyes. "Erin told me all about you," he said.

"Did she now," I said.

But he was quite friendly with me: "How you used to be a bonafide private eye! That's really great. Always wish I'd done something like that."

"Always wished I'd been a brain surgeon," I mumbled, not really in the mood to be too much of a smart-ass tonight.

"Anyway, I saw you sitting there and I told Bobby-boo," said Erin, "I told Bobbob: 'Let's invite him to our party this weekend.'"

"Indeed," said Bobby-boo, "we'd love to have you as a guest."

"It'll be fun," Erin said, kicking me under the table with her pointed toe.

Her tap hurt. I didn't let it show.

"Sure," I said, "Love to."

* * * * * * *

Love to, my ass. But what do you say when you're talking to the husband of a woman who, just a week earlier, had squirted her fuck juice straight down your throat?

Still, Saturday night came, I had nothing to do, I didn't feel like sitting around on my little boat, so I put on a dress shirt and my nice leather sports coat and walked up several docking piers to Erin and Bobby's large boat, dubbed *The Sympathy*. It was a giant, bright white beauty made by Crescent Custom: seven cabins, a large entertainment area, a sailboat the size of mine attached to the back. There was a hot tub with several naked people, drinking wine, in it. The party seemed several hours under way. Loud contemporary jazz played on the sound system—something atmospheric with the upright bass and piano. Many of the attendees were fellow boat people whom I'd seen around but didn't really know. Hell, let's face it, I didn't know anybody and I didn't know squat, which was always the problem with me, which is why I always found myself in the shit that I seemed to easily sink into.

For instance, Stephanie...

* * * * * * *

But first, there was Erin.

She spotted me, holding a tall glass of champagne. She was wearing a low-cut, sheer green silk evening gown that was practically see-through. I wondered why she bothered wearing anything at all: I could see her nipples and the hint of pubic hair through that fine fabric. Maybe that was the point, because I instantly decided this view of her was far more erotic and enticing than if she were naked like her guests in the hot tub.

"Hey," she said, "thanks for coming," and she gave me a kiss on the cheek, grabbed my hand, said, "you look good," and she moved her mouth close to her ear and: "maybe later we can slip away for some quick fun." She took a step back and said: "Have fun. Get yourself a drink, why don't you."

I started making my way toward the bar and Bobby intercepted me like we were on a basketball court. "Mr. Private Eyeball!" he said, and chuckled, first grabbing me by the shoulders and then vigorously shaking my hand. "Good to see you here! Having fun? Oh, you don't have a drink! Go make yourself a drink this instant, fellow!"

At the bar, I started to make myself a tall White Russian. A young woman appeared at my side. She wasn't any older than twenty, but what did I know. She could have been fifteen or thirty, I could no longer tell. She was wearing a pink halter top and a very mini denim skirt. Her legs were skinny and smooth and tanned. Her arms, shoulders and chest were just as tanned. She wasn't wearing a bra and her nipples were dark, pointy, and yummy. Her eyes were blue and she was a blonde (of course).

"Looks good," she said, "make me one?"

I gave her mine.

"Oh," she said.

I started making another.

"Nice," she said when she sipped it.

"Most bartenders don't know how to make a White Russian for garbanzo beans," I told the girl; "a great beverage of this ilk should always be one thirds equal parts."

"Right," she said and nodded her cute little blonde head of hair, "they usually get too thick on the milk or Kahlua and not the vodka. Oh, by the way, I'm Stephanie," and she held out her small, smooth hand.

We chitchatted, we talked; we moved about the giant yacht to places where we seemed to be alone and could talk. It doesn't matter what we talked about and I'm not even sure I remember. We did drink a number of my especially made White Russians. Stephanie said she had to pee and excused herself but then came back and said: "The women's restroom is occupied and there's a line and I really have to go, you wouldn't mind if I...*oh fuck it,*" and what she did was lifted her mini-skirt, pushed her thong panties out of the way, hoisted herself up on the safety rail, pointed her ass and crotch towards the water. She almost slipped and fell and I caught her and she said: "My knight in shining something," and holding onto me, she let it fly: a long stream of piss heading straight into the marina. No one at the soiree seemed to notice, or they didn't want to notice; Stephanie found this funny, she giggled, and I guess I found it amusing as well and laughed and the next thing I knew I was kissing her, I was kissing her as she relieved herself over the bough.

* * * * * * *

And the next thing I knew I was in one of the cabins with Stephanie, on the bed, pushing those thongs out of the way so I could get my cock inside her tight little pussy, her legs on my shoulders, the miniskirt around her hips, one tit peeking out from the halter. "Fuck me *hard,*" she said, "I mean really hard, old man," pressing her fingernails into my neck, "fuck me *good*, baby." I did my best.

"You remind me of someone," I whispered.

"Your first love?" she asked.

"No."

"Your mommy?"

"No."

"Who?"

"Someone dead," I said.

She reminded me of Rhonda Littlefield.

* * * * * * *

Stephanie and I were going at it a second time. She was sucking me off and helping me up for the adventure. Erin walked in on us. She leaned against the wall and said: "Isn't this *something.*" She said: "Isn't this a *sight.*"

Stephanie popped my dick out and said is a raspy tone: "Wanna join us, you pervert?"

Erin's dress seemed to slip off her body and she was naked and standing next to the bed. "If you don't mind, I'd like to, yes."

"Do you mind?" Stephanie asked me.

I said: "Only a fool would mind," or something like that.

I knew this was going to be a mistake but at the moment, I didn't give a fuck. Or I did give a fuck-two fucks and a blowjob, actually.

* * * * * * *

Erin got up and she suddenly had a bottle of something and plastic cups. Where did she get it? Who cared? I needed a drink like they did and so we drank and eyed each other's sweaty, shiny, fuck-stinky flesh. The two women started to lip dance all over my body. After two drinks I started to feel funny. I was dizzy, but as horny as a male finch in a cage with a dozen winged bitches. "You slipped me a fucking mickey," I said. The two women laughed. I giggled with them. I couldn't move from the bed. I was numb all over but my prick was thick and hard.

* * * * * * *

"Now isn't this a sight?" said Bobby as he walked in on the three of us. We all chuckled and pointed at him and told him to get naked. He got naked. It was then I noticed he was holding a camcorder.

* * * * * * *

I woke up and it was a bright sunny day and I felt like complete and total shit, like I had gone to Tokyo and Godzilla had stomped the crap on me for an hour and a half. I was also naked and my crotch and mouth smelled of dried pussy juice, and I'm sure most of it came from Erin. I found my clothes on the floor and put them on. Erin and Stephanie's clothes were there but no Erin and Stephanie. On the deck I found Erin and Bobby sunning their bodies and drinking mimosas. Bobby wore black Speedos and Erin was topless with a pair of thongs. Twenty feet away from them lay Stephanie, spread-eagle on a giant towel, completely nude and working on that wonderful tan. They all said good morning. I mumbled something. Erin asked if I wanted a mimosa and I said, "Why the hell not."

"Please sit down, my friend," Bobby said, patting a chair between him and his wife.

I sat and sipped my mimosa.

"Hair of the dog, eh?" said Bobby.

I couldn't reply. I shrugged.

"Quite a night," said Stephanie, sitting up, what little fat on her belly making small curls.

"Oh boy," said Bobby.

"Oh yeah," said Erin.

"Ugh," said I.

"I have something to show you," Bobby said, standing up. Did I have to see all that hair? "Please," he said, "come with me."

I followed him into the boat's entertainment center. There was a 42" Sony plasma screen. Erin and Stephanie joined us, not bothering to cover themselves. They sat very close to each other on a loveseat. I didn't like how this was playing out but I was too damn hung-over and enjoying the mimosa to give a damn.

I was ready for anything, I suppose, but I really wasn't ready for what happened next.

Bobby had a remote control in his left hand. He hit play. On the plasma was some low-lit porn, home porn, and I was the star; Erin and Stephanie were the starlets, except, when on screen, they were going at each other, which caused them, in real life, to giggle and one another and kiss: watching themselves was getting to the two women, who looked like mother and daughter at that moment, all hot-'n'-throbbin' again.

I said: "Funny."

Erin said: "Tell him."

Bobby said: "Here's the deal, gumshoe. It's time to put those ol' shoes back on and get 'em dirty again. It's time to do the voodoo that I know you do oh so very moo-moo," and he chuckled like he'd just said the funniest thing in the whole wide goddamn fucking world.

I said: "What?"

Erin said: "Tell him, BoBo."

"This," and Bobby pointing to the plasma screen that had Stephanie's lubed up hand sliding three fingers into my asshole, "is good ol' fashioned blackmail."

"Fast forward it to the *nasty* stuff," Erin said.

"Yeah," Stephanie said, playing with Erin's nipples, *"the nasty!"*

Bobby hit fast play to the part where Stephanie and I were in the bathroom and taking turns pissing in each other's respective mouths.

"Nothing like a little golden shower between complete strangers," Bobby said.

Hmm. I even remembered that part, and the memory was a good one.

CHAPTER THREE

"So what's the deal?" I asked.

"Here's the deal," Bobby said. "There's a fellow two piers down, has a really huge yacht, *The Sherry Love*. His name is Roland Wilson. Do you know him?"

"No," I said, "but I've seen the boat."

"He's an asshole," Erin said.

"Yes, a real asshole," said Bobby, "and something needs to be done about him."

"What does that have to do with me and this?" I asked.

Now, on the plasma screen, I was making Stephanie lick my balls.

"Wilson is clean, too clean on paper. I need some dirt on him. Something very, very bad. It'll have to be planted."

"And just exactly where and when do I come into the picture?"

"You'll plant the bad shit! And it has to be bad enough to ruin his reputation, maybe even make his wife leave him and his children disown his ass."

"And what makes you think I can help you with this evil plan?"
I polished off the mimosa and wanted to ask for another but knew well enough to not to.

"You're in that kind of business, buddy," he said.
I laughed.
"We did some checking around."
"We asked questions," Erin chimed in, proudly.
"We found out you didn't exactly move by the play-book for private eyes."
"You have your skeletons."
"Who doesn't," I said, and looked at Stephanie: "And where do you come into all of this?"
"She's just the hired gun," Bobby said.
"More like hired pussy," Stephanie said, opening her legs and touching her own pussy.
"And a nice one at that," Bobby observed.
I was thinking that.
"I'll say," Erin did say, running her hand across the pussy in question.
"And I don't come cheap," Stephanie added.
"We got our money's worth," Erin said.
"I think I'll be going now," I said.
"No," Bobby said, "you will sit down and listen."

* * * * * * *

"If you don't do what we want, we'll spread this tape around and ruin your life."

Well. I had a really good laugh.

I said, "Go ahead. I don't have a reputation or life to destroy. That was done long ago. You picked the wrong washed out alcoholic man for sexual extortion. I don't have a career, family, or even any personal integrity to embarrass. So send the tape anywhere you want. Hell, who knows, maybe I'll get laid more often."

"I doubt it," said Erin, "you're a drunk and not so good in bed."

"Look who's talking, Lady Leaky Faucet."

She made a face: ha-ha.

"Stephanie is young and looks even younger," Bobby said, "we could send the tape to the cops and tell them she's fifteen."

"I'm only in high school and this bad old man seduced me," said Stephanie in a funny small voice, like of like Japanese anime; she was sucking on her thumb and batting her eyelashes, too. It was a damn good acting job, I thought.

"But you're not," I said.

"It'll still cause you trouble," Erin said.

I shrugged. "I can take some trouble."

"There's something else," Bobby said, "and that's Stephanie's boyfriend."

"He's a big, jealous, mean killing machine," said Stephanie, "and let me tell you, boy, if he ever got a gander of that vid-vid, he'd hunt you down, skin you alive, and then bar-be-que your hide and feed it to the bikers who go to the bar that he owns."

"I've seen him," Erin told me, nodding her head, "and he *is* big and mean."

"And my, oh, my, quite *ugly*," Stephanie went on, "but I love him *so*."

"He knows you're a whore?" I said.

"He loves whores."

"Well," I said, taking in a deep breath.

"So what will it be, gumshoe?" asked Bobby.

"My answer," I told the three of them, "is for you to all go fuck off and die. Do whatever you want. Break a bunch of legs. *Bonne chance*, like the French say. As for me, I say: 'Fuck you very much.'"

I got up and started to walk away. I expected someone to pull a gun on me but there was no gun.

Before I parted ways with this trio of criminal misfits, I stopped and said: "Assholes."

"You'll regret this," Bobby said.

"Probably," I said, "I always do, eventually."

* * * * * * *

Returned to my boat and sobered up by drinking bottled Fiji Water for most of the day and getting more sleep. Fiji Water usually does the trick. My gut was hurting, where I'd been shot three times and healed.

I took a nap and dreamt that I sailed my boat to Fiji where I lived peacefully and happily ever after.

Night came and I wondered what Bobby and Erin would actually do. I got dressed and decided to pay a visit to *The Sherry Love*. Jesus, that was one big boat; it was an

Italian made Benetti Patricia class. Twenty cabins, an apartment building on water. Must've cost ten or fifteen million. I called up, I said I needed to speak to Roland Wilson.

I said it was very important. I was let aboard. Roland Wilson was a man in his mid-50s, very well-built and wearing all black: slacks, t-shirt, sports coat, loafers. He had a long grey beard. I'd heard he'd made his fortune in some sort of bio-tech stock deal. I met him in the dining area of the boat. He was having rib-eye steak and that steak smelled like Heaven. I was offered dinner but I declined. At his side was a woman in her early 20s, a brunette with saucer-shaped eyes and a soft white body, like she hardly went out in the sun-odd for a boat person.

"This is my wife, Sherry," Wilson said.

The boat!

"Nice to meet you," I said.

"Likewise," she said, very softly.

I couldn't help myself: I undressed her in my mind and made long, slow love to her all night and fell in love.

"To what do I owe the pleasure of your visit?" asked Roland Wilson, breaking my fantasy. "Your face is familiar, but we've never met."

"It ain't good news," I said.

"Assuming it's not."

So I told him everything—well, not everything, but enough.

"I see," Wilson said. "Well, I'm not surprised."

"He's a bastard," said Sherry.

"So there's some bad blood," I said.

"You can say that," Wilson said; "I married his daughter, Sherry, for one. He was not happy about that.

The age difference, of course. I married her the day she turned eighteen, although we'd been carrying on since she was—"

"Roland," said his wife, "please."

"Her first job was at a certain pharmaceutical company. Some information came her way, she passed it along to me, and I turned my life's savings into a fortune. What she did not, however, was share these trade secrets to her father and his wife, her stepmother. They tried to get the SEC to investigate but there simply was no hard evidence, although since the statute of limitations has since run out, we can freely admit our little insider-trading scheme. You do what you have to do...to get ahead in this world. Wouldn't you say so?"

"Sure," I said, and to Sherry: "Erin is your step-mom?"

"Do you know the cunt?"

"Language, dear," said her husband, patting her bare knee.

"I mean 'bitch.'"

"We've met."

"She hates me. I hate her. It's a simple story."

"I don't get it," I said, "you all live in the same marina?"

"We were here first," Wilson said. "Her father made some money doing what he did, day trading and that sort of thing, and he and his wife purchased a boat and specifically moved here."

"To make our lives unpleasant," Sherry said.

"Why not move?" I asked.

"Why give them the satisfaction," Wilson said.

"They're pretty bent on ruining you."

"They can try. I appreciate your coming to me with this."

"Why not. They tried to blackmail me."

"What do I owe you for this information?"

"Nothing."

"Oh please."

"Well."

"Name your price."

"Like?"

"Name it."

"Five grand," I said.

"Let me write you a check," he said.

I thought: hmm. Easy money.

* * * * * *

Check in pocket and feeling pretty damn dandy being paid about my good deed for the day, I walked back to my tiny boat. I didn't make it. I was jumped by two big guys with lousy intentions. One held me still while another knocked me on the back of the head with something quite hard and cold.

CHAPTER FOUR

The headache I had, when I woke up, was worse than the morning's hangover.

I felt a lump that had dried blood on it. I was lying on a smelly old green army cot in a narrow room filled with empty beer kegs and boxes of hard booze. A large man, his muscles going to fat, sat across from me in a white lawn chair. He had a thin moustache and long hair and I had a feeling he may have been the fellow who gave me the headache. I owned him one.

He also looked like he could've been a relative of the Martoni Brothers and didn't sit well with the three bullet wounds on my belly.

"Where am I?" I asked.

"Hey, Gregory!" the man said to the closed door.

The door opened and another big man (whose fat seemed to be turning into muscles, like he'd just discovered the world of weight-lifting three months ago) walked in. He was bald. I figured he was the one I had to settle with-I noticed a black revolver tucked into his pants. There was loud music and cheering coming from somewhere in this building. The place smelled like stale booze, piss and cheap disinfectant mixed with bleach.

"Get a good nap?" he said with a grin.

"You're Gregory?"

"And this is Steve. Steve, go get Tony."

The other man stood and left. Gregory sat in the lawn chair. I didn't think that poor piece of plastic would hold out much longer, the way it bent and made strange sounds that no lawn chair should ever make.

"What's the story," I said, "Gregory."

"You fucked up, pal."

"No kidding."

"Tony is pissed."

"Who is Tony?"

"I'm Tony, motherfucker," said the man who walked in, followed by Steve. He was around six foot five, skinny, tattooed, long black hair in a ponytail. He wore leather pants, cowboy boots and a vest. He would've been handsome if his face weren't so pockmarked. He tossed something at me and I caught it. It was a videocassette. "I watched your movie," he said.

"Oh shit," I said.

"'Oh shit' is right."

"I take it you're Stephanie's boyfriend?"

She said he was ugly and she wasn't kidding.

"Why must we resort to labels and expectations? The cunt is my property. What I want to know is what were you doing fucking what is mine when you didn't get my permission or even pay for it?"

Now I knew why Stephanie reminded me of Rhonda—these sorts of women were all the same.

With that, he came over to me and backhanded me across the face. I tasted blood. I rubbed my jaw.

"I was set up," I said.

All three of them laughed.

I said: "Really."

"Tell me about it."

So I did.

The three of them looked at each other.

And they laughed.

"It's the truth," I said.

"That's so nutty I believe it," Tony said. "Fuck it," he said, "I'm sick of this bullshit. Go get Nancy," he told Gregory.

Gregory nodded and left.

"Why am I here?" I asked.

"To rough your shit up, maybe even kill you, but now I see you're just a fucking dupe. Like Homer Simpson in *Day of the Locust*. Ever see that movie? One of my favs. Donald Sutherland was great in it. So you got caught up in the pussy game. Happens to the best of us, but mostly happens to the worst, y'know. She used to get me, Steph did. She used to get me to do what she wanted; get me all pissed off and hurt any man she had a problem with. But you know what? This is the last time. This is it. I'm not playing anymore. This time she's going down into the sea and sleeping with the fishes, like they say in the gangster movies. This time she's dug her own grave. I'm officially breaking up with her."

Gregory returned with a redhead in gold high heels and black panties and bra. She could have been twenty, or she could have been forty. She looked tired and jaded and I found myself liking that—then again, these days, I wasn't too particular about the women I was attracted to.

Tony said: "This is Nancy. She's my apology to you. So have your bad ol' self some fun and then I'll see to it you get back home."

I was left alone with the woman.

"You okay?" she said.

"Yeah," I said.

She sat next to me. "You sure you're okay?"

"Yeah."

She smelled like cheap wine and baby powder. "You want to kiss me?"

"Do I have to?"

"You should," and she leaned in to kiss my cheek and whispered: "You won't be okay soon. You're in danger."

"How?"

"Mmm, baby, that's good," she said loudly, for effect, then whispered: "We don't have to do this. I don't want to do this. I don't like seeing people get hurt, especially stupid men like you."

"I don't like seeing myself get hurt either," I agreed.

"I don't want to do this," and she added loudly: *"Yeah, baby, touch me right there like that!"*

"What the fuck," I said.

She whispered: "They always set up poor saps like you, and use me to do it. We start fucking, then Tony's goons come up and smack you around just when you're about to get your rocks off and leave you broken and bloody and naked in the street for the cops to find. It's not pretty, let me tell you, and I bet it's embarrassing as hell."

"Great."

"But that doesn't have to happen."

"It won't," I said. "Just keep up your act."

She started to moan and say nasty, sexy things. I grabbed one of the empty beer kegs and moved it next to the door. I nodded to Nancy. She yelled, "OH YEAH BABY FUCK ME DEEP!" A few seconds later the door opened and Steve came in. I picked up the empty keg and brought it down on his head. He went to the floor, unconscious. I reached for one of the booze boxes and yanked out a fifth of José Cuervo Gold. Gregory burst in next like an elephant out of the jungle. I smashed the bottle across his face and rammed the jagged end into his belly. He went to his knees, cursing my existence like a mad Catholic priest. I relieved him of his gun.

"I'll be going now," I said.

"You'll be going to hell," he said.

"Yeah," I said. "I know."

* * * * * * *

I escaped out the back exit. There were a lot of motorcycles and hot rods parked outside the building, a placed called Tony Hole with a neon sign: "LIVE NUDE WOMEN AND GIRLS." I was somewhere in Mission Beach from the looks of it. Not too far from home. I found a parked taxi and told the driver to take me downtown. It was a good thing I had a few bills in my wallet. I still had my check from Roland Wilson too. I couldn't wait to get to my boat, curl up in bed and pretend the last two days never happened.

But I wasn't going to find peace on the calm waters of the marina boat docks. There were a dozen Harbor Patrol police cars and two ambulances, and they seemed to be focused on *The Sherry Love*. I saw Sherry Wilson, a blanket covering her shoulders, talking to three police officers. I didn't want to know what was going on. I did my best to keep away from the cops, since I had a gun on me and my face and head were bloodied up.

The girl who lived on the boat next to me, her name was Jolene, was standing on her deck. She was a cute Asian girl who was always in a bikini, but tonight she was in slacks and a halter. She asked me if I knew what was going on, with the cops and the ruckus.

"The usual," I said.

"The usual what?"

"Usual standard operational bullshit," I said, "otherwise known as USOB."

"You're funny," she said.

"I know," I said.

CHAPTER FIVE

There was someone in my boat, sitting on my bed.

"It's good to see you," Stephanie said. She was wearing cut-off jeans shorts and a tank top and had no shoes.

"I can't say the same. You're not welcome here."

"Oh please," she said, standing and coming to me. She tried to cuddle; she tried to kiss. I pushed her away. "Do you hate me so?" she asked like a little girl to a big bad daddy.

"I just got away from Tony."

"I'm sorry. Things didn't work out as planned."

"What? That Tony didn't kill me or make me a cripple?"

"If it makes you feel better, he wants to break my arms and legs too, and this time he means it. That's why I gotta lay low. I gotta hide, I gotta run away. And because of what's going on out there..."

I could hear the police radios...

"What *is* going on out there?" I said.

"Bobby snapped and took a shot gun to kill Roland Wilson. But Wilson was ready and shot Bobby. So Erin snapped and went after Wilson with a huge knife and Wilson shot her too. They're both dead."

"Sounds like self-defense." I hoped so, anyway. I wondered if my check would clear. Then again, I'm sure Wilson could hire the best lawyers to iron it all out. I hoped I wouldn't have to testify. I hoped the porn tape wouldn't have to be played in court.

Stephanie said: "I don't know why I got caught up in all this."

"Money."

"Um-hm."

"Everything we do...we do for money."

"Or love," she said, "and hate."

She said she couldn't leave, she was afraid. She cried and my heart went soft—just a little, because she *did* remind me of Rhonda Littlefield. She asked to sleep here with me. She said I could have her; I could do anything I wanted as long as I didn't send her out there to the wolves.

We went to bed.

I flipped her onto her stomach and pulled her shorts down. I said: "Bad girls get it up the ass."

"I *am* bad and I want it that way," she said, "yes, give it to me that way, that's what I want and deserve."

Sure, I was going to do it, but not right away. I wanted to have a little fun first—call it a going away present. I was sober this time, I was more aware. I was able to enjoy this young woman's body. I ran my tongue along every part of her lithe tanned body, from her forehead to her toes, because I knew this would probably be the one and last time I would have the opportunity to taste such an exquisitely naughty nymph. *Carpe diem*, as the old saying goes, and I did plenty of carpe. When I got between her legs and clamped my hungry mouth on her dirty little pussy, I hoped she would squirt like Erin, I hoped I would get a full acidic taste of Stephanie, but not much luck- when she came, she came just like any other woman: with a small shriek, a shudder, and the digging of her nails into my back.

She didn't draw blood.

I wished she would. I deserved to bleed.

Instead, I drew blood from her. I moved up and took her left, hard nipple into my mouth and bit down.

"Owie-wowie," she said, and sighed, and said, "Bite me harder, Mr. Private Eyeball."

And so I did, and I tasted her blood, and her blood made my cock get very hard.

This is when I flipped her on her stomach and shoved it in her little waiting, hot ass.

"Do I get punished now?" she asked.

I said: "This is only the beginning, little bitch."

Her asshole was burning and juicy and took me in like a solider returning home to a long lost horny wife.

* * * * * * *

When she fell asleep, I made a phone call.

* * * * * *

Met him at the entrance of the peer.

Had Gregory's revolver pointed at his heart.

"You're alone?" I asked.

"I said I'd come alone, like we agreed."

"Got the money?"

"Right here."

He tossed over a wad of bills: $5,000, as agreed.

Handed him the gun. "It's not loaded anymore."

Tony smiled. "No hard feelings. Gregory had an ass-whoopin' coming to him. And because you made that call, we're even and you have a few extra dollars in your pocket. Where is she?"

"Asleep on my boat. But whatever you do, do it somewhere else. Not on my sail ride. Do it far away."

"I like you, brother. You're a coldhearted bastard. We're cut from the same cloth. I know who you are."

"Payback sucks," I said.

"It's a bitch, all right," he said.

"Yeah," I said, walking away.

"Hey, Nancy tells me you're a great fuck!"

"Yeah," I said.

He laughed and I did not.

How did I get caught with these people? How the hell did I arrive here? Where does a life like this begin, anyway?

"I said I know who you are. Doesn't that make you curious?"

"Not really," I said.

"Two years ago," he said. "Good job with those Martoni Brothers."

My skin felt like someone just tossed a bucket of pig shit on it.

"No loss," he said. "Those fat fucks had it coming."

CHAPTER SIX

Rhonda Littlefield: at the time I thought she was one of a kind, but I was learning she was one of many.

Larry Malzberg found her. Larry was a fellow P.I. I occasionally did some work with—he needed help on a case or I needed help on a case, sometime we worked well together and sometime we didn't. He'd been hired by Rhonda's parents in Oakland, California to find her; they heard she was in San Diego. He found her stripping at the downtown club owned by the Martoni Brothers. She was "free, white, and twenty-one" (her words, but I knew the movie) and told Larry her father hand wandering hands and her mother liked to torture her with lit cigarettes; she convinced Larry all they wanted to do was hurt her, so he informed them that Rhonda had took off to the island of Aruba and that was that, she would never be heard from again.

He was fucking the girl, of course.

I was at Larry's place; we were kicking back and watching some Hong Kong action movies he'd ordered over the Internet. His phone rang. "Yeah, yeah, sure, okay," he said and put the phone down. "Rhonda's coming over," he said.

I was very interested.

"Oh really," I said.

"Really," he said, and yawned.

I'd wanted to fuck Rhonda like I wanted to fuck any woman who crossed my filthy tracks. She said she had a boyfriend, but the boyfriend was never around...little did I know that her "boyfriend" was all three of the Martoni Brothers.

"She sounds whacked," Barry said.

"Good," I said.

"She drives me up the wall sometimes," he said.

"She needs to get rid of that 'boyfriend,'" I said.

"Or he needs to get rid of her," Barry said.

Rhonda arrived fifteen minutes later. She was sweaty, smelled like tequila. "Brisk walk," she said, giggling, giving us both a hug and a kiss on the cheek.

"Nice outfit, Rhonda," I said.

She was wearing a white cotton tank top and tight white shorts with the word LOOK on her ass. Her ass was hanging out of the shorts. She wasn't wearing a bra, the cotton top was see-through, especially with that film of sweat...

I imagined Rhonda walking from the motel room she lived in, that ass swaying, the sweat forming on her skin...and cars honking her.

"I like your jogging gear," I said.

"You like?" she said. "I *bet* you do," she said, looking over her shoulder and smiling at me.

"Oh, I do," said I.

"Pervert," said she.

"And what's so perverted about looking?"

*"Every*thing," she said, walking away, going: "Larry, what do you got to drink around here?"

"There's that bottle of Chivas you left last time," Larry said.

"Yum."

"You want to drink more?" he said.

"Glug, glug," Rhonda said, holding her head up, mouth open, and pointing a thumb down.

"You're drunk already," Larry said.

"I had a few," she said. "Hey, I'm young, I can drink gallons," she said.

She made us all a drink.

"Party away, boys," she said. "Hey, what were you two doing? Watching pornos and jerking off?"

"Kung fu movies," Larry said.

Rhonda rolled her eyes. "You and your funny movies, kid."

Somehow we wound up in Larry's bedroom. Rhonda finished her drink and was lying on the bed, on her stomach. I was sitting next to her, thinking about the right kind of move to make on the girl. Larry stood, looking annoyed, playing with his drink.

"I must be crazy," Rhonda said.

"Yes," Larry said, "you are."

"I must be crazy," she said, "being here with you two like this. As far as I know, *you both might kill me.*"

"Funny," Larry said. "Look at me: ha, ha."

"Ha?"

"Ha."

He seemed uncomfortable.

Rhonda turned her head to look at me and said: "Maybe just you. *You*, you might just slice up my flesh and filet me."

"You'd like that," Larry said.

"You know, I *might*," she said.

"Filet your ass?" I said, and gave her ass a soft smack.

"Mmm," Rhonda went, wiggling her butt.

I smacked it again.

"Oh," she said, "you're bad. Will you filet me now?"

"I wouldn't filet this ass," I said, "I'd just fuck it."

"Promises, promises," she mumbled.

I hit her ass, hard.

She wiggled and moaned.

"Bad Rhonda," I said.

"I'm very bad," she said, "I need a good spanking."

I smacked both her cheeks a few times.

"I need to get hand to flesh," I said, noticing a few brown pubic hairs sticking out of her shorts.

Rhonda lifted herself up as I pulled her shorts down to her ankles...one ankle anyway.

"No undies," I said, "bad Rhonda."

"I'm a bad Rhonda, Big Daddy," she said.

I gave her a few more tender slaps, then slid a finger into her cunt.

"Okay, guys," Larry said, "I'll leave you two alone."

"No, stay," Rhonda said.

"I'll just be out here," Larry said, stuttering.

I moved a finger into Rhonda's asshole.

"You're the bad, bad, bad boy," she said.

I leaned down and kissed her left cheek, slightly red from my touch.

"Was that a promise or a threat?" she asked me.

"What?"

"That you'd fuck my ass rather than filet it."

"Why don't I do both?"

"I have a boyfriend... "

"Does that matter now?"

"I mean, it's okay if you fuck my ass, but not my pussy."

"Because of your boyfriend?"

"Yeah."

That didn't make sense, but I didn't care. I managed a second finger into her asshole.

"You do have a condom, I hope," she said.

"That I have. But hang on. Don't go anywhere."

"I'm right here, Big Daddy."

"Don't call me that," I said.

"Yessir."

I went to the living room. Barry was watching TV. "Hey," I said.

"Hey," he said.

"Do you have any lube? K-Y?"

"There's some Vaseline in the bathroom. Why?"

"Why do you think?"

"Are you really going to fuck her?" Barry asked.

"Finally, yes. Don't you want to?"

"Not really."

"You can go first if you want."

Larry sat up. "Look," he said, "have fun. I'm going for a walk. How long do you need?"

"Don't know."

"I'll be back in an hour," he said, and left.

I returned to the bedroom with the bottle of Vaseline. Rhonda was still on the bed, a pillow under her hips now. She was playing with her clit.

"I made myself come when you were gone, dude," she said.

I hovered above her, my pants down, the rubber on my cock. I started to apply the Vaseline to her.

"Where's Larry?" she asked.

"Left."

"Why?"

"He needed a stroll."

"Does he hate me?"

"No."

"I wish he was here."

"Me too."

I fucked Rhonda for fifteen minutes, smacking her little butt cheeks now and then. "Hit me harder," she said, and I did. By the time I came her rear end was bright red.

I lay down next to her.

"Everything you hoped for?" she said.

I smiled.

"I see how you always look at me," she said.

"It's the way you dress."

"How do I dress? Like a whore?"

"Like you want to get fucked."

"I *always* want to get fucked," she said, "I just don't get fucked by the right men."

"What do you mean?"

"I wish Larry was here," she said, "he could fuck me next."

"He's not here."

"No, I guess he is not. So you'll have to fuck me again, if you want to."

"I want to," I said.

"You can fuck my pussy this time. My ass is sore, you fucked that too hard and it'll be sore for a week."

She giggled.

I slapped her one across the two cheeks.

She turned over on her back.

"Pussy next," she said, "I want it in the pussy."

"What about your 'boyfriend?" I asked.

She said: "The hell with them."

I was horny to catch and think about "them."

* * * * * *

I was watching the rest of the interrupted Hong Kong flick when Larry returned, two hours later.

"There you are," I said.

"Where is she?" he said.

"Asleep."

"Passed out, you mean."

I shrugged.

He sat down. "So you fucked her?"

"Three times."

"Everything you hoped for?"

I laughed. "She said the same thing."

"Whatever," he said.

"What? Why don't you want her? She wants you to fuck her."

"I know. But I don't want to."

"Why? She's gorgeous, hot, sexy…"

"She's nuts."

"Ahhh," I said, waving a hand.

"Really," Larry said, "something isn't right in that girl's head."

* * * * * * *

The next day, Rhonda called me while I was jerking off, thinking about her.

"Hey," she said.

"Speak of the devil," I said.

"What's that?"

"How are you?"

"Sober," she said. "Can I come over? We need to talk."

"We can talk on the phone,"

"I want to talk face to face," she said, serious.

"Okay," I said.

She knocked on my door half an hour later. She was wearing faded jeans and a purple tank top, again no bra. Hard dark nipples, etc. Hair pulled back in a ponytail. Bright lipstick.

"Drink?" I said. "I have vodka…"

"Tempting," she said, "but no."

We sat down on the couch, distance between us.

"Look," she said, "yesterday."

"Yeah."

"I was really drunk."

"I know."

"You took advantage of me."

"No I didn't."

"Okay, you didn't."

"So," I said.

"So I was upset about something, that's why I got drunk, and I didn't want to be alone. So I called Barry. I came over. And there you were..."

"Regrets?"

"I feel funny."

"Why?"

"I went to Larry's because I wanted Larry to fuck me."

"But not yours truly?" I said.

"Look," she said.

"Should I feel insulted?" I asked.

"Not at all," she said. "I like you."

"Well, that's good," I said with a smile.

"We're friends," she said, "and I don't have many friends, you know."

But my heart felt sad because I knew where she was going.

"You scare me a little," she said; "what I said about you cutting me up and making my meat into filet..."

"Oh come on," I said.

"I'm kidding," she said, but I knew she wasn't.

"It was nice," I said, "being inside you."

"I can see myself being in love with Larry," she said. "But he hates me," she said.

"No he doesn't," I said. "He cares about you," I said.

"Like I was a stray cat," she said.

"The thing with Barry," I started to say.

"He saved me."

"He did."

"He's afraid of women," she said. "He likes his movies better," she said, "because movies aren't real."

"No," I said.

"It's because his last girlfriend tore his heart apart," she said.

"Yeah," I said.

"I could mend that heart."

"Do you really want him that much?" I asked.

"It's a fantasy," she said. "Look, my boyfriends can never know what happened between us."

"Okay."

"Well, I don't give a crap. I'm going to break up with them."

"You're a wicked wench," I said, "a naughty slut."

"That's me, dude," she said.

"You should be treated as such."

"I should, shouldn't I?"

"Yes," I said, "and what you're going to do, slut, is lay across my lap right now, and I am going to give you what all bad girls who cheat on their boyfriends get."

"And what's that?"

"The spanking of their lives."

Rhonda stood, took off her jeans and panties, and lay across my lap.

"You better hit me really hard," she said.

"I will," I said.

Later, as she got dressed, Rhonda said, "This can never happen again, okay?"

"Okay," I said.

"Oh my ass is going to be so black and blue tomorrow," she said.

"I hope so," I said.

"This is a one time thing, okay?" she said, looking at the wall. "And I have to tell you something," and she told me who these boyfriends were: thugs, criminals, pizza makers, stripper bar owners. "They would kill me if they knew what I did," she told me, "and they'd kill you too."

I nodded; after she left the sadness returned.

* * * * * * *

Three days later, she called before midnight.

"Sorry," she said. "Asleep?"

"I'm awake."

"I didn't know who to call."

"What's wrong?"

"Nothing's wrong."

"You're calling."

"I wanted to hear your voice," she said.

"I like the sound of your voice, too," I said.

"I broke up with my three boyfriends," she said.

I wanted to say "good."

"They didn't care," she said.

"Where are you?" I asked. I could hear the sound of cars.

"A payphone, three blocks away from my motel."

"What are you doing?"

"Will you come over?"

"Of course," I said.

"Will you bend me over and spank me hard?" she said. "Will you tell me how much I'm a very bad, naughty little girl?"

"Of course," I said, "and then some."

"And this time, after you pound my ass raw," she said very softly, "I want you to make love to me."

CHAPTER SEVEN

When I got to her motel room, an hour later, Rhonda was dead. She was naked, on her bed, baggies of heroin scattered on the floor, a needle sticking out of her arm.

I called Larry.

He looked like he wanted to cry when he saw her.

"She told me about the men she works for," I said, "her boyfriends."

"They did this," he said.

"Yeah," I said.

"Do you still…?"

"What?"

"Do hits."

"I don't know what you're talking about."

"I know you double as a hit man."

I moved away from him, from the dead body. "I don't know what you're talking about."

"I have a job for you," he said. "I'll hire you."

* * * * * * *

I was no stranger to violence. The first person I killed, a woman, I was twenty-one, the same age as Rhonda. But that wasn't a hit. That was a mistake. But hit men got involved, and so did more violence, more murder, and more sex.

It was after that fatal night, after my first kill, that my life changed and became what it is today: a mess of bullets and blood…

PART II

"I don't mind a reasonable amount of trouble."
—SAM SPADE IN *THE MALTESE FALCON*

CHAPTER EIGHT

I had gotten married at nineteen to a twenty-six-year-old woman named Heather Gavin; it didn't last a year. I was an angry young man who didn't believe in love, didn't believe in anything.

On my twenty-first birthday, I drove from Los Angeles to Las Vegas in a crappy station wagon. I was divorced, alone, without any prospects; I had some money from stock options that I got as a gift when I graduated high school; figured I might as well piss it all away.

In a traffic jam on the Strip, I rear-ended a black Cadillac. A large, muscular bald man in a neon green suit got out. He looked pissed-off.

"Oh shit," I said.

I couldn't drive anywhere to escape.

The big man in green opened my door and yanked me out. He smashed my face onto the hood. I tasted blood.

"Bitch," he said, "I'm gonna kill you."

I heard a gun shot.

I wasn't the one shot.

The big man stepped back, touching the bleeding bullet hole in his side.

"Leon—in—neon!" a Rastafarian with plenty of long dirty dreds said. He was standing on the sidewalk, dressed in white leather. He was holding a handgun with a silencer.

No one on the Strip paid attention except me.

"Bitch," Leon in neon green said, "you shot me."

"Yah, and I's gonna shoot you again, mon."

The Rasta guy did just that, shooting Leon in neon three times in the chest.

Leon went down.

Red blood, like the blood that would be on my windshield a few days later.

Rasta pointed his gun at me.

"I don't know him," I said.

"I just saved your life." Rasta smiled, his gun down. "One of these days, you owe me, mon. Be ready for that day."

He turned, and walked away very fast.

There was a break in the traffic. I jumped into my car and got the hell out of there.

I went straight to the Stardust Hotel and checked into a room.

* * * * * * *

What I needed was a massage and a blowjob. I looked in the Vegas Yellow Pages and called "Dial a Perky Blonde."

I gave my Visa Card number over the phone. It was a new card with plenty of credit.

There was still blood in my mouth. I checked for missing teeth. There were a few loose ones, but I knew they'd hold in there.

The escort arrived forty minutes later. She was nineteen or twenty; blonde and perky. The hair on her head was too blonde. Her tits were small and perky. Her body and voice were also—perky.

"So," she said, "so, so, so."

"A massage," I said, "and then I'd like you to suck my dick."

"Three hundred."

"Two."

"Deal!"

"I want you to eat my cum, too."

"You're crazy," she said, "that will cost you an extra hundred—and I won't swallow it. I'll hold it in my mouth. But I'm spitting it in the sink. The world's just too dangerous to be eating the cum of strangers."

"A hundred bucks," I said, "forget it."

She shrugged.

"And I'm not wearing a condom," I said, "I don't want a blowjob with a condom, I mean what's the point?"

"No condom, an extra fifty."

"Deal."

When she left, I went down to the casino and played some blackjack.

* * * * * * *

I left Vegas with two hundred and three dollars more to my name than I'd arrived with. This was a good sign. This was a turning point. The drive back to L.A. was pleasant.

On the freeway, I called my friend Sammy on the cell phone.

"Yo!" he said.

"Sammy."

"Hey, hey, hey," said Sammy.

"I'm feeling good," I told him, "I'm feeling *real* good."

"Me too," said Sammy. "I had this great XTC last night. Not in a pill. Powder. You snort it. And—"

"You don't understand," I said, "I'm *feeling* good. No bipolar shit here. I'm feeling—positive."

He said: "Adrian is having a party tonight."

"Yeah?"

"You should go."

"I think I will."

"See you there?"

"See you there," I said, and pressed the "End" button on the cell.

He didn't even say happy birthday. Well, I didn't tell him, and I didn't expect him to know. We weren't good friends.

I had no friends, really.

* * * * * * *

Adrian's party in Santa Monica was infested with a lot of Los Angeles wannabes: indie film actors, sit-com extras, theater throwaways, budding screenwriters bullshitting about their first sale around the corner, neophyte directors who couldn't find their way out of their own assholes without a guide-dog.

The usual riff-raff.

But there I was, in fresh clothes, showered, drink in hand, chatting away with these folks. I had the smile on my face. You learn the L.A. smile fast if you want to maintain idle party-talk.

I was making myself a second drink—I was drinking Long Island Iced Teas—when I ran into Sammy.

"Come with me," he said.

I followed him into the bathroom. He had a vial in his hand. He poured some powder onto the basin and started cutting up lines.

"Wait," I said, "that isn't the snortable XTC you were talking about, is it?" I wasn't in the mood for E.

"Nah, it's blow."

"Okay."

Sammy handed me a rolled up fifty dollar bill. I bent down and snorted a line off the sink. When I stood, I looked at my reflection in the mirror. Thin long hair, a beard. Twenty-one years old and going nowhere, but I knew that was all about to change.

"What do you think?" Sammy asked.

"It's good."

"Better than usual."

A young lady in a thin emerald dress opened the bathroom door. "Ooops," she said. "I just wanted to pee." She saw the coke. "Hey, can I join?"

"Sure," Sammy said, handing her the bill.

She bent and snorted. She smelled nice, and she smelled like trouble. I decided to leave her and Sammy alone.

I had been married to a woman like the young woman in the emerald dress—the aspiring actress/model/singer/artist who loves her drugs. I was in the rut that I was in because of that marriage.

I felt something bad in my gut. The coke was making my scalp tingle.

I didn't want to be around these people anymore. I loathed these people. I fucking hated every one of them and what they stood for and all their crap and it seemed like I just couldn't get away from them; this was L.A. and there was just no getting away from them. I told myself long ago that I would stop coming to these parties.

I could get away from them now. I could take action and just leave. So what if I'd only been here for half an hour? Who would notice? Who would care? I'd rather be alone.

I left the party. I got into my car and drove home.

I was on Wilshire ten minutes later. There was a lot of traffic but traffic was moving fast and steady.

I turned on the radio.

Something jumped in front of my car. A large object. I thought someone had thrown something at my car. I hit the object with a thud. My windshield cracked. The object flew away. I kept driving. I was driving faster. What the fuck was that? There was blood on my windshield. Did I hit something that was alive? It was awfully big. Was it a person? Did I hit a person?

I turned around at the first light. I had to go back and find out what that was.

Traffic was at a still up ahead. People were gathering. On the street lay the body of a woman with dark skin—a tan, I think, or was that just the blood? She wore a dress and a coat. Her body was twisted. I'd hit her with my car all right. What was she doing in the middle of Wilshire and Santa Monica where there was no cross-walk?

I turned my car around, took a side road, and got the hell out of there.

I don't know what I was thinking. I *wasn't* thinking.

CHAPTER NINE

I parked my car at my apartment building. I inspected the vehicle—evidence of the impact was on the hood: a dent, more blood. *Blood on the windshield.*

I was fucked, and it wasn't sinking in how *really* fucked I was, and how badly I had just fucked up.

I went up to my apartment and tried to think of whom I could call about this. Like I said, I had no friends.

I called my stepfather in Palm Springs. That bastard would get a kick out of this. He didn't answer the phone, and I didn't leave a message.

I'd just returned to L.A. and now I had to leave again. There wasn't anything else I could do.

I packed some clothes.

I grabbed a spare towel.

I returned to my car. I looked around, made sure no one was watching. I was alone. I cleaned some of the blood off the hood and the windshield.

I tossed the towel into the trunk. I'd get rid of it somewhere, anywhere.

I got back into my car and drove.

I kept thinking of the excuses I'd make if a cop stopped me and wanted to know about my cracked windshield. "A rock from a bridge," I'd say, "I parked the car in West Hollywood and went to a club and when I came out, there was the cracked windshield. Must have been some kids. An ex-girlfriend did it, she's jealous, should I put a restraining order on her?"

I hadn't been pulled over by the cops since I was nineteen.

I got on the freeway and headed for Palm Springs.

There wasn't enough gas in my tank to make it all the way. I could have stopped for gas, and I would have made it to my step-father's house; but this didn't happen.

I was *in* Palm Springs, at least. My car died about three miles from my step-father's.

I left the car on the side of the road and walked. It was actually nice to walk in the Palm Springs night; this gave me time to calm down and think.

By the time I arrived at my stepfather's house, my feet hurt and the sun was beginning to rise.

I wasn't ready for a new day. I had no choice.

I thought of calling him first, but the battery had run out on the cell phone.

I sat on the curb in front of my stepfather's house and took my shoes off. My socks were sweaty and stank.

My body stank. I wanted to lay in a bed and sleep for a long time.

The birds were chirping.

A kid on a bicycle rode by, and tossed the morning paper on the lawn. The kid looked at me. I smiled and said good morning but he didn't say anything, just rode away and kept tossing papers around the neighborhood.

I heard a door open behind me. I stood up. My step-father still rose at dawn, and read the paper. I'm sure he still drank a whole pot of coffee while doing so. He was wearing an old worn black robe. I knew that robe from childhood. He was bald, and wore gold-rimmed glasses.

"Bill," I said.

He looked at me and squinted.

I walked toward him, holding my shoes. "How you doing? Good morning. I mean hello. I mean, I know this must seem weird."

"It's unexpected. What kind of trouble you in, kid?"

"Trouble?"

"You look like shit," he said. "You look like you've been through hell. You look like you're in trouble."

"Yeah," I said. "I am."

"You got that same look on your face like when you were a kid—like when you'd get in trouble."

"Can I come inside?"

* * * * * * *

He offered me a cup of coffee. I sat at the small table in the dining room. The TV was on: CNN. He was always a news junkie. He'd never gone anywhere in the world, but he liked to know about the world.

I told him about my car running out of gas and that I walked the three miles to get here.

"I haven't seen you in five years," he said. "Since your mother passed away."

When my mother died, he took the insurance money and moved to Palm Springs. I'd gotten some money, but blew it within eight months.

"I know," I said, knowing what he was getting at.

"I get a phone call—what? Christmas? Father's Day? Not even Father's Day. My birthday? No. Christmas. Once a year. 'Merry Christmas, Bill.' 'Merry Christmas, kid.'"

"Bill," I said.

"And now here you are."

"Bill," I said.

"You say you're in trouble, and you show up at my door at six-thirty in the morning."

"Bill," I said. "Look—"

"Is it money? Do you need money? I can give you some money. Not a lot, but I can give you some money if you need money because I know how it goes, I was your age once, I was poor, I know how it goes when you need money."

"It's not money."

"What is it?"

I told him about the car accident last night.

"Shit," he said, and sipped his coffee. He shook his head. "You did a hit and run."

"I didn't want to. I went back. There were people there—"

"But you left. It's still a hit and run."

"I got scared. I wasn't thinking. I'd been at a party."

"And you were partying?"

"A little."

"So what are you going to do?"

"I don't know."

"Why did you come here? Do you think I know what to do?"

"I didn't know who I could talk to," I said. "I didn't know what I should do."

He sighed and shook his head. "What I think you're going to need at this point," he said, "is a lawyer."

"I was thinking that too."

"Know any?"

"No."

"I know one here. I have an idea." He looked around, found the TV remote, turned the TV on. He changed channels to an L.A. station, morning news. "Let's see if you made the TV headlines, boy. Let's see if you're famous."

Forty minutes later, the blonde anchorwoman mentioned a Russian woman getting hit by a car on Wilshire last night. She was working at a nearby retail store, had just gotten off work. The car that hit her left the scene of the accident. Eye witness reports were sketchy, it was dark. "Los Angeles Police say that the driver probably won't be charged with vehicular manslaughter, as the Russian woman was illegally crossing the street—unless the driver was under the influence," the anchorwoman said. "The driver will be charged with felony hit and run."

I felt like I was going to be sick.

"Well, there's something, at least," my stepfather said. "You're famous."

THE YACHT PEOPLE

* * * * * * *

My step-father got ahold of the lawyer he knew. I talked to the lawyer on the phone. I told him what happened. He said he'd look into it and call back. He said to come into his office after lunch. The lawyer's name was Kurt O'Brien. He was a single-attorney outfit, one secretary, a small office downtown Palm Springs. He was in his fifties and heavy-set, slicked-back silver hair, patchy skin. I wondered how my stepfather knew him.

My stepfather drove me to the lawyer's office, and sat there with me as O'Brien gave me the "scoop."

"The sheriff made a routine stop to check out your wheels. Abandoned car, you know. Noticed the cracked windshield, the dent on the hood. And blood. There was plenty of blood on your car."

"How do you know all this, Kurt?" my stepfather asked.

"The cops told me."

"Did you tell them you knew who I was?" I said nervously.

"I told them I was representing your interests."

I didn't feel good.

O'Brien smiled. "Relax. I'm a *lawyer*."

"It's okay," my stepfather told me, a hand on my shoulder.

"They ran your plates," O'Brien continued, "get an L.A. address, your name, your car matches a description of a hit and run. All they need to do is match the blood on your car to the woman. But you did run the woman over."

"Yeah," I said.

"I called the LAPD. They shuffle me to some detective, nice guy. He says you won't be charged with vehicular manslaughter."

"That's what the news said," I said.

"Unless you were under the influence."

My voice lowered. "We have a problem there."

"Were you drunk?"

"He was at a party," my stepfather said.

"A party? For how long?"

"Not long," I said.

"Did you drink?"

"I had two drinks."

"Beers? Cocktails?"

"Long Island Iced Teas."

He whistled. "Strong stuff. What are you, five-ten?"

"Yeah."

"Weight?"

"One-eighty."

"You may or may not have been over the legal limit. Doesn't matter, that's moot. But hear me and hear me well: do *not*, and I repeat *not*, tell anyone, ever, outside this office, and especially not to the police or the D.A., that you had two of these Long Island Ices Teas. Do you understand me?"

"Yes," I said.

"What about drugs? Did you do any drugs at this party?"

"Yes."

"Oh, shit," my step-father said.

O'Brien held up a hand. "What kind of drugs? Pot?"

"Cocaine," I said. "Just one line."

"Five days, you turn yourself in. The shit will be out of your system. I'll be there with you. I'll tell them I'm bringing you in. But here's the other thing: you *don't* tell them you were at a party. You don't tell them anything. We'll say you were just driving around, clearing your head, who knows, people drive in L.A. for many reasons. But no party. Why? The L.A. D.A. will want to know where this party was, whose party. Your friends will be questioned, subpoenaed. Someone might say they saw you drinking, they saw you doing the blow. That won't be good. At no time do we want the D.A. to think you were under the influence. You'll just be charged with the hit and run."

"Will I go to jail?"

"It's a felony...have you ever been convicted of anything?"

"I've never been arrested," I said.

"There was that shop-lifting shit when you were fifteen," my step-father said.

"He was a minor, that's expunged," O'Brien said. "So, nothing? Nothing at all?"

"Traffic tickets," I said.

"For what?"

"Running a stop sign, not having my seat belt on."

"That's nothing. Okay, you have a clean record. You won't do any time, not major time. Maybe a little time, maybe some community service. You'll get a slap on the wrist we play this right, okay? This could be worse, but I'm on the job, okay?"

"Okay."

"But here's the other thing—I'll handle the matter here in Palm Springs. It's better you turn yourself in here, since your car is here. You go back to L.A., the sheriff here will get pissed. The sheriff will think you were here, then you split. He might put things together and give your old man a hard time, and we don't want that."

"No," my stepfather said, "we *don't* want that."

"No," I agreed. I knew I was being a pain-in-the-ass enough for him.

"You're arrested here, they'll transport you to L.A. I know a good lawyer in L.A., he'll do right by you."

"Okay," I said.

"Now we need to talk about money," O'Brien said. "My normal retainer is a thousand dollars, then one hundred fifty an hour. Seeing that you're Bob's kid and all, and Bob is a friend, I'll just charge you five hundred bucks; that'll cover all the running around on the phone and my time down at the sheriff station when it comes. Okay?"

"Okay," I said, and reached for my checkbook. I wondered what the lawyer in L.A. would cost me. It was a good thing I didn't lose my savings in Las Vegas.

CHAPTER TEN

O'Brien accompanied me to the Palm Springs Police Station. I turned myself in. I was arrested, and processed. I was placed in a holding cell with several other men. I didn't talk to anyone. I was given a sandwich and an apple to eat.

I had to give up my clothes for a dark blue jail outfit.

In the morning, I was transported to the court in Indio. I was to be remanded to the Los Angeles County Sheriff's department for arraignment.

"No bail?" I asked O'Brien.

"Not until you get to L.A.," he said. "Don't worry. My friend in L.A. will help you."

* * * * * * *

Two days later, I was paid a visit by one Max Waxman, a criminal defense attorney with a Beverly Hills office. Looking at his slick suit, I knew this was going to cost me every penny I had in the bank.

We sat in the attorney-client conference room in the L.A. courthouse downtown.

"How you doing?"

"I want to get the fuck out of here," I said, and I meant it.

"L.A. County jail is no picnic, I know."

"You've been in jail?"

"No." He smiled. "But many of my clients have. So let's get down to business."

"What is this going to cost me?"

"My fee will be a clean three grand if we clear this matter up today in court. Can you handle that?"

"I can. We're not going to trial?"

"Do you want to go to trial?" he asked.

"I don't want to go to prison," I replied.

He nodded. "You won't have to. You're not being charged with vehicular manslaughter. The woman had no business crossing that busy street like that. Clearly her fault, but you did flee the scene of the crime."

"Yeah."

"Yeah. Major fuck-up, and Kurt says you were under the influence at the time."

"Not by much."

"A tiny bit and you'd be fucked beyond all recognition. But your test came clean. You're going to get the felony hit and run charge, a fine, some community service, a one year suspended sentence, five years probation."

"What's a suspended sentence?"

"You keep out of trouble for the five years, you don't have to worry. Get into any trouble, you'll do the year—which means you'll probably do four months. But you *don't* want to do any time."

"No."

"So," he said, "we go into court, you plead guilty to the hit and run, you sign a shit load of paperwork, and that's that."

"I can go home then?" I asked.

* * * * * * *

The process was easier than I'd thought. There were a lot of my fellow jailhouse mates standing in line; we were like pigs heading for the grinder. I was paying Waxman three grand for this?

I'd been a man on borrowed time. I knew I deserved this.

After the judge proclaimed my sentence, a man in the pews stood up and said, "That is all? He is not going behind bars?" He had a thick Eastern European accent. "He murders my sister and he doesn't have to pay for his crime?!?"

"Order!" the judge said.

"THIS IS AN OUTRAGE!"

"Mister," the judge said, "there will be no such outbursts in this court!"

I turned and looked at the man. He was tall and muscular, swarthy; wore a beard and glasses, and he was balding. He glared at me with pale blue eyes.

"I will have justice," he said to me, "and I will make you pay for my sister's murder!!!"

"Bailiff!" the judge cried. "Remove that individual from my courtroom!"

The man went without a fight, but kept staring at me.

Wonderful, I thought.

* * * * * * *

It felt very nice to be back in my apartment. There were some messages on the answering machine. I didn't listen to a single one. I went to bed. I slept for twenty-four hours straight.

* * * * * * *

Someone was knocking at my door. Through the peephole, the short redheaded woman in white shorts looked harmless. I opened the door.

She asked my name.

I said yes.

She handed me some folded papers and told me that I had been served. She walked away. I was confused.

The papers consisted of a summons to the Los Angeles Superior Court and a complaint for wrongful death and negligent infliction of emotional distress, filed by Pieter Dragamenchenko.

The woman's brother.

He was asking for two million dollars in damages.

Wonderful, I thought.

THE YACHT PEOPLE

* * * * * * *

"I'm sorry this happened to you," Max Waxman said on the phone, "but civil litigation isn't my area of expertise. What I do is keep people out of the slammer. Your check cleared, by the way, and I thank you. I know a very good attorney who handles civil matters. In fact, she's very, *very* good. She'll do right by you. Would you like her number?"

"Sure."

"Her name's Lisa Dean. Tell you what, let me call her first. Then she'll call you, and she'll make that little problem of yours go away. Don't worry. Your life will get back to normal."

CHAPTER ELEVEN

Lisa Dean was an associate at the law firm of Fritz & Fitzgerald. She had a male secretary in a Brooks Brothers suit. I figured I was probably going to have to use my credit cards to pay for this legal counsel.

She was my age, something I wasn't expecting. I had to remind myself there were people my age running the business and entertainment world in this town. Knowing this didn't help my self-esteem.

I didn't expect such an attractive woman, either. Attractive isn't the word; beautiful or gorgeous wouldn't describe her. She was beyond sexy, *she was sex*. She was Ally McBeal on crack. I don't think I'd ever seen a shorter skirt in a business-ensemble. She didn't wear pantyhose, and her legs were southern California tanned and well-defined. The best casting director in all of Hollywood couldn't have done better. I'd just stepped into an erotic movie. Her dirty blonde hair was pulled back in a tail, accentuating her forehead and large brown eyes. Her hand was moist and warm and pulsating—when I shook it and we introduced ourselves. She looked me up and down, and took her time, and didn't hide this. She was a predator, she was letting me in on this from the start—hell, *she was a lawyer.*

"So," she said, walking towards her desk, her ass swaying, "you're getting sued."

I handed her the legal papers and sat down. I watched her carefully as she read the documents. Her thick red lips moved as she did so.

She asked: "Do you want to settle this?"

"I don't think I have the money," I said softly. "In fact, I know I don't have the money."

"I didn't ask you if you had the money, buster boy, I asked if you wanted to settle. We can offer this guy and his third-rate lawyer one dollar."

"I don't want to settle. I did nothing wrong. It wasn't my fault—the cops even said so."

"Exactly," she said. "This lawsuit is bull-fucking-shit. They just want to see if they can get any money out of you. Maybe they think you're feeling guilty. *Are* you feeling guilty?" She lowered her voice and leaned forward.

"A little."

"A little is too much. You have nothing to feel guilty about."

"The woman is dead—"

"And it was *her* fault."

I nodded, and then I told her about the threat the woman's brother made in court.

"He was talking out of his ass," Lisa Dean said. "Tell you what." She stood, walked across her office, and sat down on the leather couch. I turned and looked at her. "I can move to have this dismissed. I happen to know the assigned judge *really* well. That's always an advantage in my line of work. When you get right down to it, it's all about people, and who you know."

I'd heard that one before.

"What do you think?"

"I think it's a good idea, Ms. Dean."

She reached back and let her hair loose. The action was magical. She ran her hands through it. "You can call me Lisa."

"Lisa," I said.

She opened her legs. The skirt was riding high and she wasn't wearing underwear. There wasn't a pubic hair on her. It looked so smooth. Her pussy lips opened up and I saw, without a doubt, that she was wet.

"Let's seal our deal, attorney-client," she said, and laughed. "Strictly confidential, if you know what I mean."

I couldn't move.

"What's the matter?" she asked. She reached down and touched herself. *"Don't you want to fuck me?"*

Yes I did, oh yes I did, and without thinking, I went to her. I pushed her back onto the couch and kissed her. I shoved my hand between her legs and felt how hot and wet she was. I unzipped my pants and gave her the fuck she wanted—I wanted—right then and there.

After, she stood and smoothed her skirt down. She walked back to her desk and sat.

She said: "I'll get a hearing date for the motion, you don't need to be there. It'll be an in-chambers thing. My secretary has the necessary paperwork ready for my retainer fee. You can pay by check or credit card. Any questions, Bobby?"

"Well," I said, "no."

"Good. I'll be in touch. Have a nice day."

CHAPTER TWELVE

Lisa Dean called me three weeks later and told me that the judge had dismissed the lawsuit based on the grounds that there weren't sufficient facts to sustain the cause of action.

"It was tricky," she said softly, "but I always get my way."

I sighed. "Thank you."

"You can thank me by taking me out to dinner to-night," she said.

"Okay," I said.

* * * * * * *

I met her at an Italian restaurant in Santa Monica. I had no idea I was being followed—one never does.

Lisa Dean was already there, sitting at the table, having a glass of white wine. Men in the restaurant were looking at her. She wore another very short skirt, black leather this time, with a white blouse and black leather jacket. Her hair was down and she'd gone heavy on the make-up and perfume.

I asked the waiter for a Long Island Iced Tea and sat across from my lawyer.

"Am I late?"

"You're on time," she said. "I'm always early." She leaned back. Her blouse was unbuttoned low. I caught a glimpse of one pink nipple. She wanted me to see it. She knew what she was doing. "This is my second glass of wine. Do you know how many times I've been hit on since I've been here?"

"I probably couldn't count."

"Not once. Oh, there are the eyes all right. But this is a civilized and refined establishment. If I was in a regular bar, I would have been accosted, hit on, proposed to, and maybe even raped a dozen times over. But not in a boring place like this. I hate boring places, don't you?"

"Why'd you pick this place then?"

"The steak and lobster are to *die* for."

The waiter came by with my drink.

Lisa Dean held up her wine glass. "A toast, to a man whose now out of trouble."

"I'll drink to that," I said.

The waiter was still there. "Shall I bring a menu?" He was trying to look down her blouse.

"I'll order for both of us," she said, and ordered two plates of the steak and lobster special.

I didn't tell her that I wasn't fond of lobster.

"So," she said, leaning back again.

"So," I said.

I felt her leg against mine.

"What will you do now?" she asked.

I didn't have a chance to answer. Pieter Dragamenchenko was in the restaurant. He'd followed me here, that was my first guess. He screamed my name, said that I murdered his sister and the United States was protecting a pig like me. He had a gun in his hand.

Lisa Dean leaped across the table like a hunted animal and grabbed me. Her nails scratched my face. She pulled me to the floor, under the table.

Bullets began to fly.

Several men became heroes in the restaurant—they wrestled the disgruntled Russian man down. He was big and it wasn't easy. Someone in a tux took the gun from him.

Lisa Dean pulled me up. She took my hand and said, "Let's get out of here."

"He just tried to kill me."

"He tried to kill *us*, kiddo. That's why we need to get the heck out of Dodge!"

* * * * * *

Our hands clasped, she led me to her car, a silver Porsche. It was quite a car. My adrenaline was too pumped up to properly admire her set of wheels.

Lisa Dean was very excited by all this.

We got into her car, and we drove away very, *very* fast. I could tell she liked to drive fast.

"You sure know how to show a girl a wild night," she said, like she was out of breath.

"Do you have to drive so crazy?"

"Does it bother you?"

"Yes."

She pouted. "Poor *baby*."

She was nuts, but I didn't know how nuts, until she made a strange suggestion...

* * * * * * *

"Well, that some *something*," my lawyer said, "anyway: life doesn't have to be boring, does it?"

"What do you think will happen to him?"

"Attempted murder, he'll go away for a quite a while. I'm sure the police will want to talk to us. *You*, for sure. You were the target. Maybe I was a target, too. It's funny to think that."

"Should we go back?"

"Not just yet. There's something we need to do. There's something I need *you* to do for me. Call it a favor, for saving your life. Will you do me a favor, lover-client?"

"Sure, I guess. What?"

"Let's go to my place," she said.

"Okay," I said.

* * * * * * *

She lived in Manhattan Beach and had a great view of the ocean. I felt depressed.

On her living room floor was a naked and gagged man in his fifties. He was thin and pale and had gray hair.

"Okay," I said, "what's going on?"

"Um," Lisa Dean said, "meet Nelson Lake." She smiled at me. "I should say His Honor Judge Nelson Lake of the Los Angeles Superior Court."

"What?"

"How the hell do you think I got your lawsuit so easily dismissed? Like I said before, it's not what you know, it's who. Sometimes in the legal profession, it's who you *do.*"

I backed away. "This is getting too weird."

"It hasn't even *begun* to get weird." She was excited again, like she was being shot at. "I'm sure ol' Judge Lake here is wondering why we're back so early. See, Bobby, we were supposed to have dinner, a few drinks, maybe a walk, and I'd bring you here, and we'd get busy on the Judge. He thought he was going to spend a few more hours in the dark all tied up. Didn't you, Mr. Judgy-wudgy?"

She kicked him in the side.

He looked at her. His eyes were filled with rapture.

Lisa Dean turned to me. "Don't look so scared."

"I'm not."

"You *look* scared."

"Well," I said, "I'm not." I was.

"You said you'd do me a favor."

"What is it that you want me to do?" I asked.

"Hang on. Wait right there. I'll just be a minute or two. *Don't* you go any where."

She left.

I looked at the man on the floor. He tried to say something. I didn't want to know what he was trying to say.

I didn't know if this was a sex game or if he was here against his will.

I found that I didn't care.

Lisa Dean returned wearing nothing but knee-high leather boots. She looked wonderful naked, but at this point I didn't want anything to do with either the woman or her body.

She had an assortment of items—two whips, an enema bag, a crowbar and a camcorder.

"What I want you to do," she said, "is be my cameraman."

"Your what…?"

"You'll operate this camera," she said, "while I do some vile and horrible things to the judge."

"You have to be kidding me."

"No, I'm not."

"I don't want to do this."

"You owe me."

"This is nuts."

"No," she said, "it's kinky."

"What the fuck," I said, "I'll do it."

I tried not looking at her breasts or shaved pussy when she handed me the video camera.

* * * * * * *

I left two hours later. I just walked out. I headed down to the beach. I hated the smell of the ocean. I waved down a passing cab and went home.

My car was still at the restaurant in Santa Monica.

I'd just spent two hours taping Lisa Dean doing some very perverted, smelly, and odd things to that judge. She had the whole ordeal on tape for prosperity, I guess. She said the tapes were better than porn, they were "avant-porn."

I never felt more dirty...

The night wasn't over; before I opened the door to my apartment, I felt a hand on my shoulder.

"Hey there, mon, don't jump," a voice from my past said.

I turned around. It was the Rastafarian guy from Las Vegas. He wore a lavender suit and it looked ridiculous on him.

"You remember me, mon?" he asked. "I saved your life."

"Yes."

"You owe me for that."

"Seems like I'm owing everyone for it," I said.

"Let's go inside and talk," he said.

"Do we have to?"

"I need your help on a job, mon."

CHAPTER THIRTEEN

Inside my apartment, I asked: "How the hell did you find me? How do you know who I am? I never told you my name. I never told you a thing about me. It was such a bizarre encounter in Vegas I was starting to think it never happened."

"Your license plate, you idiot," he laughed. "I took down your numbers, I find out your name and address."

"Oh."

"My name is Gregory," he said. "I a hit man, mon."

"No kidding."

"I here in the City of the Angeles to do a job."

"And you need my help."

"That I do."

"I can't get involved in a fucking hit on someone," I said. I threw my hands up for a dramatic effect.

Gregory looked very serious. "You owe me your life, mon."

Under his jacket, I could see the gun he had in a shoulder-holster.

* * * * * *

We drove in his generic Ford rental car. I felt claustrophobic, sitting next to Gregory the Rastafarian hit man.

"This the plan, mon," he said. "My mark is inside a gay night club. My mark may recognize me—he know there is a price tag on his head. We've run into each other from time to time, y'know, and he knows what I do for a livin', y'know."

"No," I said, "I don't know."

"In a gay club, I'll stick out. He sees me, he makes a run for it, things get messy. We want this hit to go smooth, if y'know what I mean, my friend."

"No," I said, "I don't know what you mean."

"We go in as a couple."

"You and me?"

"Yah, mon."

"What, do I look gay?" I asked.

"Don't take nothin' personally," he said, laughing. "What do I know, what and who looks gay or not? We go in as a couple…"

"Great."

"You owe me."

"Yeah, yeah. I do this, we're even? I don't owe you nothing?"

"Even steven," he said.

"Tell me something," I said. "Leon in Neon. Why did you kill him? What did he do?"

"One of his wives pay me to kill him, mon," Gregory said. "Ol' Leon was a bigamist."

"You knew him?"

"We crossed paths."

"Do you often 'cross paths' with the people you kill?"

"Not

I nodded.

* * * * * * *

The club was in West Hollywood. I'd heard about the club. It was popular and had display lights in front. I could hear the music inside—thick on the bass, very danceable.

Gregory took my hand when we walked up to the entrance.

"Just don't kiss me," I said.

"You too ugly to kiss, mon."

He paid the twenty-dollar cover charge, and we went in.

It was like any other club: dark, smoky, loud; the smell of sweat and anticipated sex glued to the brick walls.

There weren't as many patrons as I thought. But it was getting late. I hoped that Gregory's "mark" had gone home.

I wasn't that lucky. Gregory spotted him.

"There he is."

The mark was a man in his mid-thirties, well-dressed and good-looking in that L.A. gay sort of way, sitting at a table with two other men, just as well-dressed and good-looking.

Gregory nudged me. He'd told me what I was to do. I had no idea if it would work or what kind of assistance I'd be contributing to the proposed death of this man.

I did it, anyway.

The man's name was Ralphie. He looked up as I approached and he raised an eyebrow.

("You need to distract him so I can make my move," Gregory had told me.)

I smiled and said, *"Ralphie!"*

"Do I know you?" he asked, and smiled.

"Ralphie!" I said again. I sat at his table. The other two men stared at me, confused.

Ralphie was confused too. Was I a one-night stand he didn't recall? Was I good-looking enough to be someone he'd know? I had decent clothes on, at least—I'd put on my best for the dinner date with Lisa Dean.

"It's been a long time, Ralphie, a real long time," I said, wondering how my acting was.

"I'm afraid I don't know who you are," he said, amused.

"You don't remember me?"

"No."

"But Mr. Kenneth remembers you, Ralphie mon." Gregory's voice was loud.

Ralphie looked up and said, "Oh fuck."

I moved away from the table, fast.

Gregory had a gun with a silencer. He put three quick bullets into Ralphie's chest.

One of the men at the table went for a gun beneath his jacket. Gregory shot him once in the head.

The second man grabbed me by my jacket. He turned me around and punched me in the jaw. I tasted blood.

Gregory shot him twice.

I spat out a tooth.

"Let's go," Gregory said.

No one tried to stop us.

* * * * * * *

I was rubbing my bloody gums, lamenting about my lost tooth. My jaw was throbbing. Gregory was driving the rental car at a legal speed. He was a man who never worried about anything.

"You did good," he said.

"It's over?" I said.

"Oh yes, your night is over."

"This has been the longest night of my life."

When he dropped me off at my apartment building, he said, "Next time, we do lunch. I buy you a drink or somethin', mon."

"Don't take this personally," I said, "but I'd rather never see you again."

He laughed. "I understand, mon. But if you ever want to get into the business of carrying out hits…"

* * * * * * *

The night still wasn't over. There was someone waiting for me in my apartment. He was a big man, and he was sitting on my couch, holding a spiral-bound notebook and drinking from a fifth of Gordon's vodka.

"Don't be alarmed," he said.

"I'm not," I said. "How did you get in?"

"Your back window was unlocked."

"You're here to kill me," I said. "So just do it. I'm ready. Kill me. Maybe I deserve it."

Pieter Dragamenchenko stood up. He was drunk, his eyes were red. It looked like he'd been crying.

"Yes, I wanted to kill you," he said in his slurred accent. "I tried killing you and that bitch lawyer tonight…"

"Yeah," I said. I didn't know what to do here.

"I got away. They called the police but I got away. I went home. I knew the police would come for me there. My mother was waiting up for me. My sister and my mother, we all lived in the same small apartment, coming here to America."

I knew this; Lisa Dean had told me.

"My dear mother, she finds this." The big Russian tossed the notebook my way. I quickly caught it. "Go ahead, you look."

I opened the notebook, waiting for Dragamenchenko to pull out a gun or knife and end my short unhappy life.

The notebook was filled with a lot of small handwriting, all in the Russian alphabet.[*]

"I don't know how to read this," I said.

He was crying now.

"She was dying," he said. "You didn't kill her. *She killed herself!*"

---

[*] Yes, this is where I got the idea of taking the blank notebook with me when I killed the Martoni Brothers.

It took a while; the Russian explained to me that his mother had gone through her departed child's belongings and found the notebook, a diary. In it, she wrote about coming to the United States, getting a job in Los Angeles, and then seeing a doctor. She wasn't feeling well. She was told she had leukemia, and the disease would kill her in a year or two. She couldn't face telling her family, or having to get treatments with enormous hospital bills. She was very depressed, but put on a face for her family: all was well and she was happy. She knew she had to end her life, and mapped out her plan in the diary: she would step into the busy intersection at Wilshire and Santa Monica. She'd seen many accidents there before. She knew it was a cowardly way to go, but she was getting sicker and there was no other way.

It wasn't my fault.

All this guilt, everything, and it wasn't my fault.

That bitch.

"Oh shit," I said.

The Russian still had tears in his eyes. "I am sorry for trying to hurt you."

* * * * * * *

I helped Pieter finish the Gordon's. I had a bottle of Skyy and we drank that too. The alcohol hurt my bleeding gums, but the pain soon faded to numbness.

The irony didn't escape me. If the notebook had been found sooner, many of the things that happened to me would not have happened.

If I hadn't gone to Vegas…

If I hadn't gone to Adrian's party…

If I'd left the party two minutes later, or earlier…

I told Pieter these things, and he nodded, and we drank.

I looked out a window and almost laughed. "This has been the most insane night of my life," I said.

"The sun is almost up," said the Russian.

"It's nice," I said, "daylight."

"Yes," he said, "yes, it is."

After that, I did think about being a hit man, or maybe a private eye…

PART III

She was an adolescent sex fantasy sprung to life.
—CARTER BROWN, *THE PORNBROKER*

CHAPTER FOURTEEN

I had wanted invisibility and a quiet life, living on my little boat, but I wasn't going to get it now.

I was the Big Name, the Celebrity, the Private Eye Who Solved the Crime. Now everybody, his brother, dog and kitchen sink wanted to be my best buddy.

Everyone wanted to buy me drinks at the yacht club. Who was I to say no to free flowing booze? I had to tell the story time and time again, and soon I got good at truncated, short versions. Sometimes the versions changed—I embellished, I lied.

I was lonely there on my boat. I just wanted to be left alone to work on my pulp stories. But I couldn't be alone. So I'd get dressed and go to the Yacht Club and come back with some random woman.

That didn't last long.

I didn't think it would.

After a few weeks, I was no longer the fuckable hero. I was just another drunk with a boat.

No one wanted to fuck me anymore and frankly, I didn't care.

I just wanted to disappear.

Forever.

But that was just a lofty wish. Hell was going to find its way back to my door again.

And maybe even a little Heaven...

* * * * * * *

I'd hoped never to see Tony's face again.

I guess I always knew I would. It what's New Age types call cosmic inevitability.

It'd been six or seven weeks since that night he took Stephanie.

The fucker showed up at 10 a.m. in the morning with espresso lattes and blueberry muffins. And a big shit-eating smile.

He let himself on my boat and woke me up.

"Rise and shine, Mr. Gumshoe."

"What the fuck," I said.

"A man should always wake up before eight o'clock," he said, going, "Tsk, tsk, tsk."

"What the fuck," I mumbled, looking at my feet and toenails and wondering if he was here to make me a cripple.

"Are you awake?" he asked.

"I am now," I said.

"And some espresso," he said, "and a muffin. It's good for you. We need to talk."

"Do we need to?"

"I have a job."

I took one of the espresso lattes and a muffin.

"A job," I said.

"I want to hire you, asshole."

* * * * * * *

We sat on the deck. The sun was too fucking bright this morning.

Tony smoked a skinny cigar, wearing sunglasses. He looked very cool and clichéd there on my boat, the sto-gie-toting gangster.

"It's Stephanie," he said.

"I was about to guess that," I said.

"That little bitch is more trouble than she's worth," he said. "Or is she? She's quite the piece of ass, as you know. So maybe she is worth it. Who knows? I can ask myself that question all day. She is what she is: the hottest cunt in town."

We sat there.

"So what is it? What did you do, Tony?"

"Me? Nothing. She's gone."

"What?"

"She disappeared. She escaped."

I was relieved, and it must have shown.

He eyed me suspiciously, and took a bite out of his own muffin.

"What's the matter?" he asked.

"Frankly," I said, "I figured you killed her."

He stared at me. He was insulted.

"Why would I kill the slut?" he said.

"Well," I said, shrugging. Did I need to say it? I didn't need to say it.

He laughed.

"You're funny," he said.

I didn't feel comic at the moment, despite my penchant for the typical P.I. smart-ass mode.

He finished his muffin and wiped his mouth with a napkin.

"I was pissed and she was due for punishment," he told me. "But it's really all psychological," and he pointed to his temple, tapping his skull with a finger. "You make them believe you'll break their arms or knock out their teeth make force them to get ass-fucked by a huge horse dick. But you never do it. But you make sure that at any moment, it *could* happen. It could."

He sighed.

"But murder a whore who makes good money, I'd be crazy," he said. "So what did I do? I stuck her in a cage. Naked, in a cage, for weeks, down in the basement. I fed her scraps and water and when I was feeling generous, I let her out and gave her a hamburger and a beer and let her suck my dick while I smacked her face. Yes, she needed to be punished, and a few months in the cage would do her good.

"But the slut was clever. Somehow she broke out. She found some clothes. And she took off."

I nodded.

He said: "I sent some men to see if she was staying with you. They watched your boat."

Worried, I said: "She's not here. She never was here."

"I know."

We stared at each other.

"I have no fucking idea where she is," I said, and, lowering my voice: "I don't care. She's caused me enough trouble."

"I know," Tony said, "but I want you to find her."

"Find her."

"It's what you do."

"It's what I used to do."

"It's what you do," he said.

"I wouldn't know where to look," I said.

"It's what you're good at," he said.

I knew I couldn't say no.

"Sober up and think about it," he said, standing up. "I'll send over a gift later on."

"A gift?" I asked.

He smiled.

"Oh, you'll *like* my present," he said.

"I'm sure I will," I said, just to be cordial.

"I *know* you will."

CHAPTER FIFTEEN

"Hey, soufflé."

I was dressed and about to leave my boat when Nancy showed up with two bottles of Korbel champagne and an envelope stuffed with one hundred dollar bills in her purse.

"For you," she said about the envelope with bills, "and for us," about the two bottles.

"Well, well, well," I said.

"Were you going somewhere?" she asked.

"Nowhere special."

"Need an escort?"

"More like a chaperone."

"How about company?"

"You got the alcohol," I said, "why go anywhere when we're here?"

She got close, wiggling her hips and giggling like a girl.

"When you're here, you're there," she said.

She kissed me. Her lipstick tasted like strawberries and somewhere else. Her perfume smelled like a life I never had but always wanted. I was convinced I could also smell her pussy.

"Are you wearing panties?" I asked her.

"Never," she said.

We went into the cabin. She worked on opening the first bottle and I looked in the envelope. I counted the bills: $5,000. Another five grand.

The cork popped and she let out a yelp. The cork bounced off the cabin wall and ricocheted, almost hitting me in the head.

"Trying to kill me?"

She looked around and said, "Have any champagne glasses?"

"Are you kidding me?"

"What do you have?"

"Plastic cups," I said.

"Ugh," she said.

"Ugh?" I said.

"Ugh," she said.

"Plastic cups it is."

So we drank Korbel from plastic cups and I re-counted the bills and thought how nice cold hard cash always looked to the weary eye.

* * * * * * *

Nancy and I were on the second bottle and kissing. Her lipstick was smeared and I had her tits out and was pinching her nipples.

"Harder," she said.

"How hard?"

"Hard as you want?"

I pinched those hard pink things harder but I was afraid to hurt her.

"Oh just let me suck that cock," Nancy said, "I need something in my mouth right now."

* * * * * * *

I had her legs on my shoulders and I fucked her very slowly. I wanted to make it last. I wanted to feel her all night. She was sopping wet, coming all over my cock again and again.

"Like that, like that," she whispered, "just like that."

"Just like that," I said.

Just like that.

* * * * * * *

After two hours of fucking, we took a break and thought about going out to get more booze. There didn't seem to be anything else important to accomplish this evening, and being an alcoholic dick, more booze seemed quite essential to my job description.

"So you're taking the gig?" she asked.

"Seems so," I said. "I mean, after a fuck like that…"

"And many more," she said.

"I would expect nothing less."

She was excited now. "Where do we start?"

"We?"

"We. I come along for the ride. Not as a detective."
She giggled. "I'm three holes for you to pump your semen
into."

"I like the sound of that," I said and I did, actually.

"Yeah," she said. "So where do we start?"

"That's a damn good question. First, I need a
drink."

"Sounds like a good place to start as any."

"It always is," I told her, just like that.

CHAPTER SIXTEEN

The first logical place to start was Los Angeles, as much as I hated going north and returning to that cesspool of ugly days and memories.

Like me, Stephanie was from the city, born and raised. She had worked "The Scene" there, according to Nancy.

"That's where Tony first found her," Nancy said, "a year ago. She was blowing disgusting old men for this series of amateur DVDs. There wasn't any man that girl wouldn't put inside her mouth and eat. The little cum rag. But Tony was smitten by her. He was investing in this company and saw her on a lot of the product and told himself he had to have her. And what Tony wants, he gets. He bought out her contract and moved her down to San Diego…and the rest I'm pretty sure you know."

"Um-hm," I um-hmmed.

"Or do you want all the sordid details, blow by blow?" She said that with an enticing lick of her lips.

"I'll leave it to my imagination," I said.

"You do have a nasty mind," she said.

"I've been trying to clean it, but the more I try, the dirtier it gets."

"Can I be your maid?"

"Can I afford you?"

"Probably not."

* * * * * * *

First, we needed a car. I didn't drive anymore; it seemed like a waste of money and time, and I already had two DUIs haunting me like the dead souls of a terrorist attack, not to mention the Russian's sister: it didn't matter if she committed suicide, to this day I still felt it was my fault, and every day I thought: what if she hadn't walked out into the intersection of Santa Monica and Wilshire to die, what direction would my life have taken? Maybe I'd have some corporate office job, with a wife and three kids at home in an Orange County suburb?

We rented a Ford Taurus with a full tank of gas and made our way to L.A. before noon.

I almost asked Nancy to get behind the wheel but she shook her head no and said she couldn't deal with L.A. traffic either.

So I drove…slowly.

We got to L.A. in three hours.

115

* * * * * *

Stephanie's sister, Sonya, lived in a small apartment in North Hollywood, off of Erwin Street. There was very little in the apartment, the place didn't look like she spent much time there; it was practically empty except for a futon and a large plasma screen TV.

Sonya was eighteen months older than Stephanie, and looked a lot like her sister except her hair was shorter and dyed purple. She didn't have the same tan as her sister, and her breasts were a little bigger. Other than that, they could have been twins of some sort—twins in my head, oh my nasty fantasies.

Sonya wasn't happy to see the two us, complete strangers, when Nancy and I arrived.

In fact, when we told Sonya why we were there, the girl said: "Fuck off, freaks!" and slammed the door shut.

Nancy and I looked at each other.

"Hate it when people are rude," I said.

"The hell with that," Nancy said. She started to knock on the door. *Bam-bam-bam-bam-bam.*

No answer.

Nancy knocked harder—BAM, BAM!!!—and kicked the door.

"You dumb skinny bitch!" Nancy yelled. "What the fuck, baby duck? You don't give a shit about your own flesh and blood?"

Sonya opened the door; she was holding a steak knife. "Leave me alone," she said.

Nancy looked at the knife and laughed. "What, you think you're *tough?*"

Sonya lunged at Nancy. I was afraid Nancy would be cut. But Nancy slapped the knife out of Sony's hand and then she smacked Sonya a good one across the face.

I was impressed.

"Bitch," Nancy said.

"Beyotch," Sonya said.

They stared at each other like one of them was going to die. I waited for the worst. They just glared. I had no idea what to do. I'd never found myself in a situation like this, and I was surprised: as a world-weary drunken gumshoe and occasional assassin, I was certain I'd been in every goddamn situation possible.

"What do you *want?*" Sonya finally asked.

Nancy looked at me. I was the man with the answers.

"We need your help," I said. "We're trying to find your sister and we thought…we thought you could be of assistance."

I felt stupid, that's for sure.

"Have no idea where she is," said Sonya.

"You're lying," Nancy said.

"She's not *here*. She wouldn't come here. Why would she? It's the first pace people would look. You're at my door. And I don't want her coming here, anyway."

"Bad blood?" I asked.

"I love Steph," Sonya said.

"Can we come in?" Nancy asked.

"You're holding the blade," Sonya said.

* * * * * * *

Nancy and Sonya apologized for getting badass on each other. They even hugged. It was a sweet second between the two.

Nancy and I sat on the futon and Sonya got us some bottled water to drink. I noticed Sonya had a slight limp.

"Sprain your ankle?" I asked.

"Born this way," she said, "my left foot is one inch shorter than the right. When I'm out in public, my left shoe has a one-inch platform so I walk like a normal person. When I'm behind the camera, no one gives a shit about that missing inch."

"Unless it's an inch on a cock," Nancy said.

"The less inches the better. I'm not into big cocks. What's the deal, anyway? You have to have ten inches or more to be a stud? I'm a small girl; average guys are just fine but average guys don't work in the biz."

"So you're in the 'biz'?" I asked.

She gave me a "well duh" look. "What do you think, hot dog?"

"You know Tony?" Nancy said.

"I never liked Tony much but I know he's what she needed," Sonya said, leaning against the wall and looking at us.

"'Needed'?" Nancy said.

"A daddy."

"Oh," Nancy said, softly. "Doesn't everyone."

Sonya smiled. "I get it. You're one of Tony's kept whores too?"

Nancy didn't reply.

Sonya turned to me. "And you're one of his thugs."

"I'm just looking for Stephanie."

"Why?"

"That's what I get paid to do."

"A thug. A thug and a whore. Typical day in L.A., eh? So what are you going to do? Break her arm and smack her around for leaving that bastard? And you expect me to help you find her? You two have some nerve."

"Look," I said, "as far as I'm concerned...okay, look, I just want to find her and make sure she's all right. As far as I'm concerned—"

"You said that."

"If she doesn't want to go back to him, I'm not going to make her."

Sonya turned to Nancy.

"Your sister is a friend," Nancy said, "I want to make sure she's all right. Something about all this... doesn't click."

"Here's the truth," said Sonya. "If Stephanie had split, she would've called me. She would've come here. She would've *told* me. But she hasn't. So something *could* be wrong. Now you have me worried."

I asked: "Is there anybody, anybody at all that your sister would go to, see, talk to, for help?"

"The only person I can think of is Captain Boner," she said.

"Captain Boner," I said.

"Yeah."

"*That* fucking pervert?" Nancy said.

"You know him?" Sonya asked.

"I know *of* him."

"You ever work for him?" Sonya asked.

"No."

"Steph and I did. We did *a lot* of work for him. He's the first pornographer who gave us jobs. Jobs that we wanted to do anyway. There are a lot of scary people in this town. There are a lot of creeps and freaks and sick bastards with cash to throw around and there's always some dumb and hungry skank who will do that crazy shit so they think every girl will."

"I know," Nancy said.

Sonya looked Nancy up and down and said: "You *do* know."

"I don't know anything," I said, a tone of mock defeat in my otherwise strong and confident voice.

"He's big and dumb," Nancy said.

"Looks it," Steph said, raising her brows.

"Thanks girls," I said.

"Anyway," Steph said, "Captain Boner was nice, he paid us well, we did a lot of work for him…and Steph went and fell in love with the fucker."

"Really," Nancy said.

"Yeah," Sonya said.

"That's…" Nancy shook her head.

"I know," Sonya said, "but he was okay. I had fun. You want to see the first video we did for him? It's really cool."

Nancy and I looked at each other.

"Sure," I said.

"I *bet* you do," Nancy said, smiling at me.

"He looks like a perv," Sonya said, "like all men."

I smiled like a fool.

CHAPTER SEVENTEEN

Sonya put a DVD into the machine and played it on the TV.

The colors were very bright. I'd never seen a Captain Boner porno, nor had I ever heard of him until today. He was the dirty old man type—rich guy in his late fifties fucking young women on his yacht.

Yeah: *another* yacht person. The world was full of them, and I started to get really annoyed and envious of these lucky mother-fuckers. What did they have over me? What didn't I have that they did?

Money.

It's always money.

Really. I sat there and watched this video and this Captain Boner was not the best-looking man in the world.

First of all, he was pushing sixty; his head was bald (he hid it with his Captain's hat), his body looked like he once worked out but was going to flab, the hairs on his chest and crotch were going white, and he made the most annoying sounds...and yet he was able to pay and fuck beautiful, young women like Stephanie and Sonya.

There was nothing remarkable about the video—it opened with Captain Boner walking along the beach, he sees two girls in bikinis (yes, the sisters in question), talks to them, and convinces them to come back to his yacht and, "hang out and party...nothing bad will happen...I'm not a dirty old man...I swear..."

The girls look at each other, smile, and go: "Okay!" Typical "reality show" style porn. I have to admit, though, it was *enticing* porn. There's something about getting older and getting off on watching a man of grandfatherly years stick his cock up (legal, mind you) teenage girls.

As we watched, Nancy's hand reached over and grabbed my leg. Her hand moved up toward my crotch.

I was getting hard, and Sonya took notice.

"You like?" she asked.

"Not bad," Nancy said.

To me, she said, her voice going an octave lower: "You *like* watching me get fucked in the ass by that old fart?"

"Actually," I said, "yeah. It's...not bad."

"Good," Sonya said. She came around the couch and joined us. She sat on the other side of me.

It all happened fast, like it was destiny—I grabbed the girl and began kissing her. She rubbed my cock under my pants. I turned and grabbed Nancy and started to kiss her; Sonya unzipped my pants, took my cock out, and went down there and gave me one glorious blowjob.

I took hold of Sonya's hair and pushed her deeper, made her take me whole, made her gag, as I continued to kiss Nancy.

"Fuck her face," Nancy said, "I want to see you fuck that little horny bitch's face."

I pressed Sonya's head more. She choked. She spat up saliva. She did not complain. The rougher I got, the more she seemed to like it.

I let her hair go.

"Get out of the way," Nancy said. She climbed over me and went after Sonya, pulling the girl's clothes off.

Once naked, Sonya lay back on the couch, her legs spread, as Nancy got a mouth full of shaved pussy.

I took note that Sonya had one nice little cunt, with little lips. It was obvious on the video, more so in the flesh.

Speaking of the video, it was still going as the three of us were at it.

I got behind Nancy as she licked Sonya to delight. I pulled Nancy's pants and panties down to her knees.

"Do it," Nancy said.

I took her from behind, first in her pussy, and then slipping it into her ass.

Sonya came several times.

So did Nancy.

"My turn," said Sonya.

The women switched—I fucked Sonya from the rear while she went down on Nancy.

We did this sort of thing for the next hour and it was nice, as far as threesomes go.

CHAPTER EIGHTEEN

Next: we paid a visit to Captain Boner.

The name of his company was called Bone Her Hard Moving Pictures, and all productions were made on his yacht, moored in Marina del Rey. Like Sonya, the boat was far more impressive in person than on DVD. It had five cabins and a small helicopter on a pad in the back, West Continental make.

What the hell have I been doing all my life, I thought. I should've been doing this shit, not chasing down cheating husbands and hunting the gutter for skip tracing gigs...and killing people now and then. But I'd come to a point in my life where I knew it was futile and stupid to envy people for what they had; because no matter how many possessions, cash and status and sex any one person could obtain, they were most likely still fucked up inside their souls.

Nancy walked onto to boat and our eyes were given some eyeball candy...Captain Boner was in a middle of a shoot. He wasn't providing much direction, mostly watching as a cameraman with a Canon XL 2 was taping a three-guy-on-one-girl scene.

It was quite a sight—because the three men were all beefy studs with ten or twelve inch cocks and the girl was quite petite, Asian, and taking a giant dick in every hole.

"Yikes," Nancy said, "that hottie can *stretch.*"

I tilted my head, so I could see the two huge dicks in both her pussy and her ass.

"Yep," I said.

Captain Boner—wearing a Hawaiian shirt, Bermuda shorts, flip-flips and his captain's hat—turned and considered us. He checked out...as for me, he shook his head: he did not approve. I agreed with him.

"Keep going," he told the cameraman.

He walked over to us.

"Sonya called and said you were on the way," he said. "You are...?"

We introduced ourselves.

"You can call me Captain Boner."

"Love your work," Nancy said, being flirty the way whores do in front of pornographers.

He took her hand and kissed it. "Why thank you, pretty lady."

The small Asian girl was screaming loud, getting fucked harder and harder every passing second.

"Let's talk where's it's a little more quiet," said Boner.

* * * * * * *

We walked down to the galley. Boner didn't ask but poured us both a glass of Chivas Regal on ice. I didn't mind at all. Nancy was polite, and sipped hers. I relished the bourbon.

We sat down.

"So Stephanie has gone missing," he said.

"We're looking for her," I said.

Boner stared at me, trying to figure out who I was.

Nancy took my hand and said, like she was a worried mother, "We're concerned. Her safety is at risk."

"Yeah, well, she was one wild little fuck, always getting into trouble," said Boner. "She *and* her sister. Gosh, I loved working with those girls. Still would…yes, I still would. But my slate is full. The world is full of hot little meat lining up for the Bone Her."

I finished the Chivas. "I bet."

"More?"

"Please."

Boner poured us both some more booze.

"But I don't have her," he told me. "Wish I did, but I don't. If that's why you're here."

There was something in his voice that didn't ring right. Something in my gut told me: this guy is lying. But I wasn't listening to my gut, and it's three bullet wounds. I was more into the taste of the Chivas on my tongue.

Nancy asked: "Do you have any idea where she might have gone?"

Boner took a moment to think.

"Not at all," he said. "I haven't seen her since she became the property of that ass-wipe in San Diego."

A tense moment.

"You know Tony?" I said.

"Only by reputation," Boner said. "Are you his 'man'?"

Another tense moment.

Nancy gave me a kiss on the cheek. "He's *my* man."

"Lucky guy."

"Thanks," I said. "Want her?"

He eyed Nancy. "I might."

"Oh," said Nancy, not knowing what to do.

And then, the small Asian girl walked into the galley. She was naked and covered from head to belly in thick globs of semen; it was in her eyes and on her nose and lips. She smelled like a cum rag.

I found her to be very sexy.

"Baby," Boner said.

"Baby," she said, her voice mocking his, "I need to take a quick shower and get all this jizz off me."

"Say hello to my guests."

She said: "Hi."

Boner said: "This is my new starlet, Sandra Boise. She is one *nasty* whore."

"I'm a whore who needs a shower before I get all *crusty,"* she said.

"Go on," he said.

She left, going to one of the cabins.

Boner looked proud. "What do you think?"

"Nice," Nancy said.

He turned to me. "Nice?"

"Very nice," I said.

"Want to fuck her? Everyone has to have some Asian food now and then."

CHAPTER NINETEEN

Little Sandra Boise returned from her two-minute shower, toweling off her tight, brown, compact body.

She stopped and eyed the three of us.

"What?"

Boner said: "I want you to fuck this man here."

She licked her lips. "I *could* go for some more dick," she said.

"You want dick twenty-two hours a day," said Boner, laughing like a fool.

"Twenty-three," she said; "who needs sleep when there's so much fucking to do in this bad ol' world?"

* * * * * * *

Nancy and Captain Boner watched, doing the grab ass thing while I fucked Sandra Boise on the galley table, sipping Chivas Regal the whole time.

The small Asian woman lay on her back on the table, her legs high in the air, as I pounded it into her.

She *was* quite a screamer.

I saw Nancy holding Boner's cock in her hand, stroking it. But that's all she did; she didn't suck it, she didn't fuck it, all she did was grasp it and Boner didn't seem to want anything else.

The two cheered us on, though.

"Fuck her, fuck her good."

"Fuck me hard," Sandra told me, and I tried my best.

The Chivas helped the mood.

"Not inside me," Sandra said.

I pulled out and came on her stomach and little tits.

"Neat," said Sandra.

"Bravo!" said Nancy.

"Damn," said Boner, "I should've got that on video!"

I caught my breath and had some more bourbon.

Sandra pouted. "I want more sex."

"Care to go for it again, friend?" Boner asked me. "This time, I'd like to shoot it."

Having already suffered the repercussions of fucking on film, I said, "No thanks."

"I'm up for it," Nancy said.

* * * * * * *

Nancy and Captain Boner agreed upon a price.

She was going to be featured in one of his videos. "You're a bit older than I usually like them," he told her, playing with her now exposed tits.

"Gee," she said, "thanks."

She didn't take it too personally; she was a pro after all.

"But you're too damn sexy to pass up."

"Thanks."

"I mean it, sweetheart," he said, and I believed him.

"I'm fucking *horny,*" Nancy said, "and I want to fuck *right now.*"

The four of us went topside, where the three well-hung studs and the cameraman were sitting around and drinking mineral water.

Nancy licked her lips, looking at those men.

"Ohhhhhhh, boooooooooys," said Boner, "ready to go another round?"

The three men eyed Nancy. They all nodded their heads.

"Then let's do it," said Boner.

I sat down and watched. Sandra Boise sat in my lap, naked herself and still smelling like sperm despite her shower.

Nancy got undressed and the three studs each popped a little blue pill and went to work on Nancy.

Like Sandra, she took one in each hole.

"She takes a big dick good," Sandra told me.

"Don't they all?" I said.

"It's not as easy as you'd think."

"You're a small girl."

"Small girls are used to gaping wide."

Boner was directing the action, holding the bottle of Chivas in one hand, sipping away as he gave orders. He was a lazy director but what does it take? The cameraman had to take a piss to Boner turned to me and said, "Why don't you come and be the cameraman for a while?"

"Me?" I said. "Nah."

"Yes."

"Go on," said Sandra. She got off my lap.

What the hell. I took the handheld cam and started shooting Nancy getting three-holed. She was loving it. It was different when looking in the viewfinder.

Then something hard hit my head.

Sandra screamed.

My hair was wet.

Nancy and the three studs stopped what they were doing.

I turned around. Boner had smashed the Chivas bottle on my head. I felt dizzy, almost fell down, but I was okay.

Boner held up the jagged edge of the bottle.

"You are *supposed* to pass out," he said.

"That only works in bad movies," I said.

We swung the jagged glass at me. I slapped it out of his hand and smacked his across the nose with the camcorder.

Next, I had him down on the deck and was pounding away at his face, cursing and spitting and loving every minute of this violence. It'd been a while since I felt so alive.

The three studs were terrified, surprising for boys with such muscles and cocks. They grabbed their clothes and ran off the boat.

Sandra watched, her mouth hanging open.

Nancy yelled at me: "Stop! You're going to kill him!"

I stopped hitting Boner. Both his eyes were swollen and he was missing a few teeth. He was conscious.

"Please," he said, spitting out more teeth and blood.

The cameraman returned, saw what was happening, and went back down into the boat.

"Why did you attack me?" I asked.

"Because you're an asshole," he said.

"I never did anything to you."

"Snooping around," he blubbered, "looking for that cunt. She's never been anything but trouble. I'm glad I sold her!"

"You what?"

Silence.

I raised my fist.

"No more, please!" he cried.

"Tell me about Stephanie."

"She was here."

"And?"

"And…"

"And?"

"And I *sold* her," he said.

"What the fuck do you mean, you sold her?"

"I sold her, you stupid asshole."

I hit him in the nose.

"Oh shit," he said.

"You're going to tell me everything," I said, "and I mean *everything.*"

CHAPTER TWENTY

That night we flew to San Francisco.

Sandra Boise wanted to come with us. She was scared and she said she had nowhere to go. She'd been living with Captain Boner on his yacht for the past two weeks.

I didn't want her to join the party but Nancy did.

"We have to," she said

"We don't have to do shit," I said.

"But she has nowhere to go."

"She'll survive."

"But Boner may take it out on her."

I didn't like the sound of that.

"And I'm sure she'll be grateful...I know you like the little chink."

But the world is full of them. Yet I gave in. So the three of us went north.

We dropped off the rental car and got a Southwestern flight.

* * * * * * *

We picked up a new rental car (that was just like the other) at SFX. It was getting dark. The girls were tired and so was I. We found a cheap motel near the airport to crash.

We slept in the same bed, of course. It was a big bed. But there was no sex. We just slept, until…

Somewhere around two a.m. I woke up and both of them were down at my crotch. Sandra and licking and sucking at my balls while Nancy had my cock in her mouth, tugging away, trying to get it hard.

I was hard fast.

And I came.

Sperm rolled out of Nancy's mouth and down to my balls, where Sandra lapped it up.

Next, I went down on them both.

First, I ate Nancy's pussy while Sandra played with Nancy's tits, and then my ass, and as I was getting a mouthful of Nancy, Sandra started sticking her tongue up my ass.

"What are you doing?" I said.

"You don't like?"

"Why don't you ream my ass," I whispered.

"Okay," she said.

So we switched. I went down on Sandra as Nancy got to work on my butt.

CHAPTER TWENTY-ONE

In the morning, we had breakfast at an I-Hop and then got back to work.

We drove to the Bay and found a yacht owned by a man known only as Mr. W. This was all based on information provided to us by Captain Boner.

What we found was something I did not expect, and made me wonder how the world really works.

Mr. W's yacht was a floating mansion. It had twenty staterooms and towered over any boat around it.

"Wow," Sandra said.

"Um," I umed.

"Wow," she said again.

"Where the fuck do these people get their money," I muttered.

"You don't want to know," Nancy said, like she knew.

A tall, beefy man in a suit—a guard—greeted us at the gangplank. He wore shades.

"Hi," I said.

He didn't reply.

"We're looking for Mr. W," Nancy said.

"He's been expecting you," the guard said, and let us on board.

We walked.

"I don't like this," I said.

"What are they going to do?" Nancy said. "Kill us?"

"They might."

"This is so *cool*," Sandra said. "I want money like this someday!"

"We're just here for Steph."

"These people deal in the buying and selling of flesh," I said, "like Tony."

She nodded.

Flesh…yes…it was all over this boat. Half a dozen women were on deck, sunning themselves or milling about, drinking juice and eating fruit and vegetables laid out on several platters. They were all naked. They were all very beautiful. They were all under twenty-five years of age. They all wore studded dog collars.

Lounging in a leather chair was a bald man in his late 40s. We wore a white robe, opened. He was naked. One of the women was sucking him off as he drank orange juice. He had a great tan and plastic surgery; the best money can buy.

He spotted us and waved us over.

"Three mysterious guests," he said.

I said: "Mr. W, I presume."

"Are you the nasty thug who opened a can of whoop ass on my old friend, Boner?"

"He had it coming."

"He's had it coming for a long time."

I noticed two more beefy men in suits standing off in the distance.

"Don't worry," Mr. W said, "you're safe here."

"Nice digs."

"I think so."

"Wow," Sandra said.

"Please, sit down. Help yourself to some—"

I said, "We'll stand. We're here for a quick visit. We came to pick to Stephanie. My employer will reimburse you the sale price."

"I can't help you," Mr. W said.

"Can we at least see her?" Nancy said. "Just so we know she's all right."

"I'm afraid you can't. She's no longer here."

"She ran away?" I said.

"My dear sir," Mr. W said with a chuckle, "none of my slaves here are forced to live this life. Take a good look around. We are in a bubble, a bubble I created with my family's wealth that goes back to the birth of this fine nation. I take good care of my slaves and—just a moment, I am about to come."

He groaned, grabbed the head of the woman who was sucking him off, and came in her mouth. She was a redhead.

Mr. W handed her an empty champagne glass.

The redhead spit the semen—and there was a lot—into the glass. She stood up. A blonde walked over and took the glass and drank the seed down with one gulp.

"Kinky," Sandra said.

"And healthy," Mr. W said, looking Sandra up and down. "Where was I? Oh, yes, I take good care of my slaves and they live a life without want or need. They don't have to work, worry or cry from loneliness. They are all loved. Why would they want to return the world?"

He had a point.

"But you bought Stephanie from Boner," I said.

"Yes."

"Where is she now?"

"I re-sold her."

"To?"

He smiled at me.

"To?"

He said: "Are you going to beat the information out of me like you did Boner? I would advise against it."

His two men took three steps forward.

"I don't feel angry today," I said.

"It's a nice day."

"We just need to find her," Nancy said.

"Hmmm." Boner looked at Nancy, and then Sandra. "The information comes with a price. All this orange juice, I need to piss. I never waste my piss. Usually one of my slaves drinks it. But if one of you two fine young ladies will take my stream, I will tell you where Stephanie is."

I sighed. Yes, I *sighed.*

Nancy and Sandra looked at each other.

"Oh I'll do it," Sandra said, "I like golden showers."

She approached Boner. She got on her knees. He opened his legs.

"Come here, sweetheart, don't be afraid."

"I'm not," she told him, "let it fly."

He held his flaccid cock in one hand.

"Get your mouth closer. I don't want too much spillage."

She moved closer and opener her mouth. He began to piss. Sandra didn't flinch, she'd done this many times. She drank him. Some rolled off her chin and onto the deck.

"Oh yeah," Mr. W said, "oh yes."

Nancy looked at me.

I raised a brow.

It was kind of sexy, given the situation, here on this giant yacht, naked sex slaves and leg breakers in suits standing around.

When he was done, Sandra took him in her mouth.

"That a girl," he said.

She stood up, and wiped her lips with her hand.

"You have a citrus taste," she said, "you're one big orange."

"Vitamin C is vital at my age," he said.

"Okay," Sandra said, "I did my part."

Mr. W turned to me. "Nice slut. Is she for sale?"

"I'm not in the game," I said.

"Where is Stephanie?" Nancy said.

"By now, in Aruba."

I said: "Aruba."

He said: "Aruba."

"What the fuck."

"I re-sold her. To a very fine Dutch gentleman. He was spending some time here and he fell in love with her."

"What is it with this Stephanie chick?" asked Sandra. "Does *everyone* fall in love with her?"

"Seems so," I said.

"Did *you* fall in love with her?" she asked me.

I didn't reply.

"I wish someone would fall in love with *me,*" she said.

"That would be easy," Mr. W said. "Very easy. You drink well."

"Thanks a tanks."

"Perhaps you could stay here? There's room."

"Wow."

"You could."

She thought about it. "I'd rather go to Aruba," Sandra said.

"If you go to the island and try to gain an entry into my Dutch friend's world," said Mr. W, "you will need the password."

I didn't like his smile.

"And what will the password cost?" I asked.

He pointed to Nancy. "A blowjob from her."

Nancy shrugged. "Why not."

She went to him and got down on her knees.

At least he didn't want me to do it.

CHAPTER TWENTY-TWO

Back at the motel room, I called Tony and gave him the news.

He wasn't a happy camper. He yelled something I couldn't understand. Then he said, "You have to go to Aruba and get her back!"

"I can't go to Aruba," I said.

"What do you mean you 'can't'?"

Nancy and Sandra were on the bed fondling each other's tits and listening to my conversation.

"Yes you can," Nancy said, softly.

"Aruba is our *destiny*," Sandra said.

"Who's that?" Tony said on the phone. "I heard Nancy. Who was the other chick?"

I explained it to him.

"What?" he said.

"Yeah."

"Is she hot?"

"Oh yeah."

"Smokin'?"

"Burnin' and Asian."

"You talking about me?" Sandra said, after she released one of Nancy's nipples from her cute little mouth.

"Look, I'm covering everything for you," Tony said. "I'll wire some more money your way."

"You really want her back that bad," I said.

"That I do, my friend."

"We need passports."

"Not a problem. You'll have them by tonight, under fake names or your real name."

"You can do that?"

"I *know* people. They'll connect me with the right person in San Francisco. I'll wire the money, you and the girls get some traveling clothes, get yourself some tickets and head on down to that island and get my slut back."

I hung up the phone.

Nancy and Sandra were naked by now, fingering each other's pussies.

"Well," Nancy said, "are we going?"

"Yeah."

They both looked happy.

"And," I said, "the three of us are going shopping."

"Shopping!" Sandra squealed, like she just came hard.

PART IV

"I'm a very smart guy. I haven't a feeling or scruple in the world."

—PHILIP MARLOWE IN *THE BIG SLEEP*

CHAPTER TWENTY-THREE

Three days later, we were on Aruba.

The little island in the Caribbean Dutch Antilles had been getting some bad press the last few years, with young women mysteriously disappearing (which had been happening all the time, but when a European girl with royal blood vanished, the world press covered it), figured to be captured and sent off to Venezuela or Arabia to live the life of white slavery; hence, the tourist trade was down so our flights and accommodations were cheaper than I anticipated.

I should've felt like the luckiest gumshoe in the world, being paid well *and* with an entourage of two horny beauties at my side.

I *should* have.

But I just felt like shit. I wanted nothing more to be back on my boat and writing pulp stories about private eyes, zombies and space aliens, drinking alone and being left alone.

But like the song says: you can't always get what you want.

Armed with my women and half a dozen Hawaiian shirts, I promised myself that if Stephanie wasn't here, if she'd been sold again, I wasn't going to chase her around the world anymore.

* * * * * *

Our bogus passports got the three of us through customs at the Queen Beatrix International Airport in the city of Oranjestad, no problem. The guy Tony found in Walnut Creek, outside the City, did excellent work—the best I'd ever seen in my career.

From there, we took a long cab ride to one of the many island resorts in the southeastern city, San Nicholas. Our lodgings were right on the beach, a comfy cottage perfect for three people on a mission.

We spent Tony's money well.

Nancy and Sandra wore flower-print skirts and halter tops, no bras, their nipples hardened with excitement. Once in the room, they quickly got out of their clothes and hopped n the extra-soft bed and began going at it.

I made myself a Bloody Mary from the wet bar and watched.

They stopped.

"Don't just glare," Nancy said, "join us."

"Let me see a little more."

The two got into a 69 position and began to lap away at each other's hair pies. I finished my Bloody Mary, felt the urge in my blood, got out of my clothes and sandwiched myself between them.

The Caribbean. Money. Sex. Wasn't this life?

* * * * * * *

"I want to *spend* my entire life here," Sandra Boise said.

Little did she know that almost happened—for her, for Nancy, for me. But I'm getting ahead of myself.

* * * * * * *

The first thing to do was track down this Dutch guy, Hans vanderMeer.

"He won't be hard to find," Mr. W had told me, after Nancy blew him and she spat his come in a glass for one of his slaves to drink. "He always moors his boat between Baby Beach and Bachelor Beach."

Perfect names. Both beaches were east of San Nicholas.

I went out on a reconnaissance mission alone. The girls were asleep in the bed. I took a taxi. Both beaches were right next to each other. I asked the taxi driver if he ever heard of a man named Hans vanderMeer and he said, "That be is boat right there."

He pointed out toward the ocean.

Another gigantic yacht, at least $20 million worth.

These yacht people were making me sick.

I sat on the beach, near a hotel, at a table and under an umbrella, while a waiter kept bringing me Mai Tais.

I watched dinghies go to and come back from the yacht several times; men, women, no one who looked like Stephanie.

Finally, I asked my waiter if he knew anything about the boat and the people on it.

"Very curious indeed," said my waiter. "A rich man."

"Aren't they all."

"With boat like that, wealthy and powerful."

"Hans vanderMeer?"

"I do not know his name, but I have heard stories about the parties on that ship."

"Parties?"

He lowered his voice. "Sex parties."

"The best kind," I said.

"That would depend," he said, "if you are a guest or you are…a worker."

* * * * * * *

I called Tony long distance. He may have been in San Diego but he sounded like he was on Mars, the connection was that bad. I gave him "the scoop," as we like to say in shamus lingo. I was very detailed, down to how good my Mai Tais were.

"Do what you gotta do to attend one of the parties," Tony said. "Do you need more money?"

"I still have plenty." Maybe I should've asked for more? I hate it when I'm honest.

"Then hop to it."

"What if Stephanie isn't on the boat?"

"Well, find out. Then we'll take it from there."

Nancy and Sandra were admiring the ocean view.

"What's up?" Sandra said.

"Shopping time again."

Sandra ran to me and hugged me.

"I love you, sweet sugar Daddy!"

"What are we shopping for this time?" Nancy asked.

"We have a party to go to."

"I *love* parties," Sandra said.

CHAPTER TWENTY-FOUR

Four things I needed, and they were easy to purchase.
First, evening gowns for the ladies, and a tuxedo for me. Mr. W had given me the low-down on the dress code for vanderMeer's parties. Next, a gun. From a cab driver and $500, I was able to obtain a .22 caliber Walther PPK.

Mr. W had told us that the Dutch man's sex parties were held twice a week. The next would be tomorrow evening.

"The pass code is usually always the same," Mr. W had said. "The word is 'hand-picked.'"

"And what if it's changed?" I'd asked.

"Then you're not going to get passage."

Now we just had to wait for tomorrow.

* * * * * * *

Something always happens to foul up a good plan.

Sandra went out for a stroll on the beach that night and she never returned. At first, Nancy and I didn't think much if it. We drank Bloody Marys and fucked and lounged on the bed and looked at the moonlight on the ocean waves.

At three a.m., Nancy woke me up and said, "She still hasn't come back."

"Huh?"

"Sandra Boise is gone, I think."

I have to admit, it was a little weird. "She's probably partying in a bar," I said. "She met a guy, or several guys. She's young, she's pretty, she's wild, and this is probably the first time she's ever been out of the country."

"That's what I'm worried about."

"Worried?"

"Yes."

"Listen to you."

She made a face. "You're right."

"Go back to sleep," I said.

"Fuck me first?"

I obliged.

* * * * * * *

She wasn't there in the morning.

Over breakfast, Nancy said: "Something is wrong."

"Maybe," I said, "maybe not."

"I can feel it in my bones."

"You sound like a parent."

"She's young enough…"

"Yeah?"

She groaned. "To be my kid sister."

"I'm sure she's just fine," I said, "she's asleep in some bed with a Dutch or German or French stud."

We ate in silence.

I didn't believe my own words and I was thinking the worst too.

* * * * * * *

I checked around.

I asked hotel stuff, bar staff, tourists: "Did you see a sweet Asian girl, so high, wandering around last night?"

Everyone said no.

But I didn't have time to worry about Sandra. There was the job, and the job always came first, right?

Right.

* * * * * * *

I felt like James fucking Bond, in my tuxedo and hidden Walther PPK, Nancy is an evening gown, all decked out and on my arm.

Mr. W had told us exactly what to do:

Find the man in a tuxedo and sunglasses waiting by a dingy to go to vanderMeer's yacht….

We walked on the beach and did so.

Give him the pass code.

I did.

"Hand-picked," I told the guy in a tuxedo.

He nodded. I was relieved. Then he put a hand up. "The lady must be naked," he said. "No women are allowed to wear clothes."

Nancy didn't object. She quickly got out of the dress in a fraction of the time it took her to get it on. She removed her panties and shoes. The man in the tux took these items and said he'd give them to her when she returned.

Another man in a tux then took us on the dingy and toward the moored yacht.

"I'm cold," Nancy said.

I held her close to me.

"I'm scared," she whispered.

CHAPTER TWENTY-FIVE

Islands in the stream...

As we approached the giant yacht, I started to get a bad feeling in my gut. The old intuition never failed me before, and I was listening. The three bullet wounds were talking: *don't do it, don't do it!*

We were far away from the United States; anything could happen out here.

Mr. W could have set us up, a bit of revenge for my beating up his pal Captain Boner.

Disco music was coming from the boat. It got louder as we got closer and I knew it was going to give me a headache.

We were escorted form the dingy and onto a yacht by a beautiful, tall blonde with a shaved pussy. Yes, she was naked.

All the women on the yacht were naked, just like the scene on Mr. W's boat.

There were, perhaps, sixty guests, twenty women and the rest men. All the men wore tuxedos; they were America, Cuban, European, South African. They each seemed to have a slave, or a companion, and were taking turns passing the women around.

A gentleman with an English accent approached us, looked Nancy up and down, and said: "Excellent piece of property."

"Thank you," I said.

"May I?"

He held out his arm, toward Nancy.

Nancy and I glanced at each other. We knew the game. She looked down, like a good submissive.

"Have fun," I said.

He took Nancy's hand and the two of them disappeared downstairs somewhere into the gut of the boat.

I knew she could take care of herself and would probably give some fun. She wanted to come along on this adventure.

Alone, I was free to wander about. Men and women were dancing, drinking, getting high on coke, fucking on the desk. This was true bacchanalia.

I wish the music wasn't so loud. The DJ was a naked, tattooed woman with short black hair.

I got myself a vodka tonic from the bar when I was approached by a man in his 40s, silver-haired, with a goatee and glasses' he wore a shiny leather tuxedo, and held a naked girl on a leash and collar. She kept behind him, her eyes down.

I knew the girl. *Stephanie.*

I didn't let it show.

The man shook my hand. He had a thick Dutch accent. "Greetings. Welcome to my home on the water. We've never met."

"But we have some of the same friends," I said.

"And who might that be?"

"Good friends," I said, "the discreet kind."

"Of course."

"You must be Hans vanderMeer."

"That I am. I see you are admiring my new slave."

"I'm admiring her very much. And I'm impressed."

Stephanie quickly looked up, her eyes met mine, she didn't show that she knew me; she looked back down.

"Would you care to sample her?" said vanderMeer.

"Oh, I would."

"Then she is yours, for now. After, let us talk."

* * * * * * *

Stephanie led me to one of the staterooms. I wondered where Nancy was, and tried to devise a plan on how I was going to get the three of us out of here. I had no fucking idea. I was, as always, winging this shit.

I needed more booze.

Once inside the room, Stephanie's face lit up. *"You!* What are *you* of all people doing here?"

I bowed. "Your knight in shining armor, m'lady."

"What?"

"I'm here to rescue you."

"Rescue me?"

"You do want to leave, don't you?"

"Why? I have everything a girl could want, *except clothes*. Do you know when's the last time I wore a pair of pants? A dress? A bra?"

"I know you're been passed around, from Boner to Mr. W to here."

That hit a nerve.

She sat on the bed and I sat next to her.

"I'm just *meat,*" she said. "I can live with it. But what the fuck are you *doing* here, in goddamn Aruba?"

I told her Tony had hired me and I'd been tracking her.

"Tony," she said. *"He's* the reason I'm here."

"He feels bad," I said.

"Does he love me?"

"He says so."

"I still love him, I suppose. But what can I do? Hans owns me now. I can't just leave."

"Yes you can."

"How?"

"I'm working on that."

"You're fucking crazy."

"Tell me something I don't know."

"You came here alone?"

"No. Nancy is with me."

"Nancy. Nancy?"

"You remember her."

"Of course I remember. Where is she?"

"Fucking one of the guests."

"Don't we all," Stephanie said. "Speaking of which, we should bop. Get your pants off."

"We need to get out of here."

"We need to play the game. We don't fuck, Hans is gonna think something is weird. And you liked poking me, if I remember."

"Yeah," I said.

She laid back and opened her legs. She touched herself. She said, "My pussy is still good. Has a lot of miles on it. Not blown out yet."

She made a good point.

When in Rome, I thought.

I got out of my tux pants and I was hard. She didn't even need to suck me. All I wanted was to be inside this hot little bitch. I could see why Tony loved her and Hans and the other men wanted to buy her.

We were just getting started when someone came into the room and knocked me over the head.

Stephanie yelled: "WATCH OUT!" but it was too late.

Not again, I thought.

And blackout...

CHAPTER TWENTY-SIX

Woke up, my arms and legs chained to a pipe. I was somewhere below the yacht, I supposed. It was dark but I knew I was still on the boat.

"Hey," a voice said.

I knew that voice.

"Sandra Boise," I said.

She was also chained to a pipe, across from me. She was naked. And next to her was Nancy. Nancy seemed to be asleep.

"He's awake," Sandra said.

Nancy opened one of her eyes. The other was bruised and swollen shut. "Hey, hey," she said, weakly.

Both women had been roughed up.

"When I get my hands on that Han's neck," I mumbled.

My head was throbbing and my brain was on fire from the knock on the skull.

"Some rescue attempt," Nancy said. "He was on to us the whole time."

"They kidnapped me as I was walking down the beach, minding my own business," Sandra said. "They smacked me around and asked me a lot of questions about you but I didn't say a word! I swear. Then they all fucked me. And more men fucked me. About thirty guys fucked me, all night, all in a row…"

She said this breathlessly and if I didn't know any better, I would've said she enjoyed getting gang-banged by thirty thugs.

Maybe she did. What did I care?

"Are you okay?" I asked her.

"Been better."

"Nancy?"

"I'll live."

"But *will* we?" Sandra said. "What will they do with us? What are we going to do? How are we going to get out of this?"

I said: "Working on that."

* * * * * * *

A few hours later, Hans came down with two of his men in tuxedos. He was holding my Walter PPK in his hand.

"So," he said, "are you a government agent?"

I laughed.

One of his men kicked me in the gut.

"This is no laughing matter," Hans said.

"I'm nobody."

"You come here, you have the password, you have women who will do anything sexually...a good cover."

"I'm just a guy. And I think Mr. W already told you."

"He did."

"So you know why I'm here."

"I find it hard to believe you came all this way for one piece of whore meat. When there are so many to choose from. The world is full of them. Why that one? Yes, I find it hard to believe."

"Me too," I said. "But here I am. I'm a schmuck who can't turn down a buck."

"How unfortunate for you."

"How about undoing these chains and letting the three of us go?"

"Hmm," he said. "No."

"People will miss us. They will come looking for us."

He laughed at that.

He said: "Who?"

And then he left.

There was a long silence.

"Are we fucked?" Sandra asked.

"Working on it," I said.

* * * * * * *

The girls were fucked.

Literally. They *got fucked*. Every now and then, some men would come down—I don't know who they were—and have their way with Nancy and Sandra. There wasn't much they could do but sit there and take it. Nancy was quiet and Sandra made noises of pleasure and even came. She wasn't faking it. She liked being held captive.

I couldn't watch. I just closed my eyes.

The best way to get through it all was to think of other times, better times, of lives that never existed…people long gone.

* * * * * * *

They didn't feed us much. One of Han's naked women would come down now and then with a cup of water and some bread. They would hand feed us.

I had no idea how long we were down there. Days, weeks. Maybe just days. All I knew was hunger. And the need for booze. Sandra and Nancy cried for food, and soon they stopped crying.

As for going to the bathroom, I won't even explain that humiliation.

Every now and then, Hans would come down, sneer, laugh, and leave.

There was no point in asking him to set us free.

We were his now.

"What will we do?" Nancy said.

"Tell each other stories," I said, "help the time to pass better…"

"Stories."

"Been thinking of a girl named Heather," I said, "someone I was once married to…"

* * * * * * *

Oh yes, I remembered things—maybe you can say my life was flashing before my eyes. I don't know what it was about that year on Kitchen Creek Court, a cul-de-sac in suburban Pasadena, California, where I grew up. Where Heather was. Oh, Heather.

Heather Gavin, when she was fifteen, wrote this in her diary:

> *I always knew there something odd about Mr. Scroggins ,the way he would look at me. I knew when he was staring from his window but I always pretended it wasn't true because I didn't <u>want</u> it to be true. He was staring at the other girls too. He was (is) very creepy, and now history has proven just how creepy he was (is).*

Heather Gavin was my stepsister's best friend; she had long, straight red hair and slightly crooked teeth, freckles and blue eyes. I should note that I was eleven at the time, a skinny kid with thick glasses and droopy corduroy pants, and a terrible crush.

It was the beginning of summer when nine-year-old Natalie McCord went missing. The McCords lived at the end of the cul-de-sac and Bernard Scroggins, a reclusive widower in his early fifties, lived next-door to them. There were three McCord children, Natalie was the youngest; I remember her as an energetic and happy little girl with long red hair. One morning, her mother and father discovered she was not in her bed, and the window of her room had been pried open. Kitchen Creek Court was invaded by the police and news vans. Bernard Scroggins had taken his motor home out to the desert for five days and when he returned home, he acted very shocked by all the attention the cul-de-sac was getting—he was seen on Channel Fifteen saying, "Oh this is just awful, just awful, I feel bad for the McCord's," but he was sweating a lot and looked nervous. The cops noticed this and they suspected the neighbor. It wasn't until two weeks later that Natalie's body was found in the eastern desert, in a place called Hemet, and all evidence pointed to Bernard Scroggins.

It was the talk of the town, not only at school among the kids, but the parents.

"To *think,*" I heard my mother say to my father, "that psycho child molester has been living among us all this time."

"You never know about people," my stepfather said, "you just never know about people."

Alone in her bedroom, the lights dim, my stepsister said to me: "I *knew* there was something very weird with that man."

"How did you know?" I asked.

"Heather told me. She said he would *watch* us."

My heart warmed hearing Heather's name.

"I heard he *raped* Natalie," my stepsister said.

"First he raped her, and then he killed her," I said.

"I heard he also raped her *after* she was dead."

"Where did you hear *that?*"

"People are saying things."

It was probably just rumor because the gruesome details, the truth, were never mentioned in the newspapers, on the evening news, or on the televised trial.

Mr. Scroggins quickly went court; my father said he probably invoked his right to a speedy trial so the prosecutor wouldn't have enough time to get a solid case together.

"It's an old defense lawyer's trick," my stepfather told me in confidence, "so the D.A.'s office will make a dumb mistake while under pressure."

Scroggins was our summer obsession. We would look at him all day on TV, watching his trial; he never said a word, his face was stone-cold—even when the prosecutor showed pictures of the decayed and mummified Natalie McCord, the girl's head caved-in from a blow by a hammer. We would talk about Scroggins at the dinner table, what was true or not, how the trial was unfolding, until my mother would say, "Enough! We are all trying to eat food, okay?" Sometimes, at night, I would go to my sister's room and talk to her about Scroggins. Heather was spending two or three nights a week in my stepsister's room, and I went there more for Heather than the courtroom drama speculations. But when Heather was there, many times my stepsister wouldn't let me in. "Go away!" my stepsister would yell. I wanted to know what was happening behind that door, certain I was missing out on something important and ritualistic.

"Let me in," I'd plead.

"Go *away,* you creep," Heather would say, breaking my young heart every time.

"We'll talk tomorrow," my stepsister would promise.

By early September, Bernard Scroggins was found guilty and given life in prison without the possibility of parole; school was just starting up and the pregnant woman who lived across the street, Sharon Burton, disappeared. She and her husband were in their late twenties; they owned a small restaurant in Anaheim and always had smiles on their faces. "They seemed like the perfect young couple," my mother said, "so happy, so promising."

"You never know what goes on behind closed doors," said my stepfather, "and that's the one true thing you can count on in this life."

My mother's theory was that someone who wanted a baby—to keep or sell—kidnapped Sharon Burton. She was apparently "snatched" while walking her dog three blocks away. The dog was found wandering around a park. My sister and Heather thought she ran off with a clandestine boyfriend. "The baby was not her husband's baby," said my stepsister, "she has a lover, the lover impregnated her, she's with him now, and they'll raise their love-child and live happily ever after." The police, however, suspected the husband—whose name was Randy—of foul play; the news and gossip on the block was that his alibi didn't quite make legal sense.

Heather Gavin said to my stepsister one night: "I bet he has girlfriends, *lots* of them," and she would write in her diary:

When I look at Randy Burton, I feel funny and my crotch gets wet. This has been happening since I was they first moved here a year ago. If only he knew! But he will never know now, since he's been arrested and it looks like maybe he did it. He's a good-looking man. He is, as they say "a handsome devil" and he may very well be a devil. I don't mind if he is a devil. I have always enjoyed looking at him...his face, his hair, his teeth, his body. I know he works out. His wife and any girlfriends he has are very lucky. If he wanted to, I would make love to him all night and be his girlfriend.

* * * * * * *

"How did you know what was in her diary?" Sandra asked.

"Later, when I married her, I found her diary and peeked," I said.

"Bad boy," Nancy whispered.

"Go on," Sandra said, "what happened next?"

* * * * * * *

As it turned out, Randy Burton did have a handful of paramours, all of whom went public after his arrest, after his wife's headless body was found near Santa Monica Beach, a dead baby girl still inside the womb. One of Randy's girlfriends was five months pregnant, she said Randy had promised to marry her and she had no idea that he was already taken. Another girlfriend was a stripper in Long Beach; she said to the press: "I always pick the wrong men, and he's another one, and I'm sorry for all the people he's hurt."

When Sharon Burton's body was found and the matter was on the news, Randy stepped outside his house and met with all the TV crews camped on the street. I stood on my front lawn, holding my sister's hand; we listened and watched. Heather joined us. I fantasized that she held my other hand and squeezed it, letting me know that she, like myself, had a covert love-feeling that could not be uttered.

"I have lived with the charade too long," Randy Burton said to the cameras, "and I confess before the world: I murdered my wife. I didn't want to be married, I didn't want a baby or this house and I never wanted to live in this godawful suburban cul-de-sac! This is not *me*, you hear?!? *This is not my life!"* He pulled out a metallic semi-automatic hand-gun and placed it to his head. Gasps.

I tightly gripped my stepsister's hand; she said, "Ouch, let go," and held Heather's hand instead, making me jealous in a number of ways.

"Randy, no," said Heather, softly, dramatically, *"no, you're too pretty to do it..."*

The police arrived, on cue. They had their guns out. "Don't do it," the cops said.

He tried, but his gun jammed. The police wrestled him to the grass, punched him in the nose, called him names, and handcuffed him. And took him away.

Heather wept as if someone, or something, had passed away.

"Crazy stuff," said my stepsister.

"Let's go inside now," said my father. I didn't even know he was there. He put his arm around Heather, told her everything would be all right, and hugged her to his side. She looked up at my stepfather and smiled.

It was just after Christmas when Heather Gavin disappeared. My sister was the only witness; the police came and talked to her. Heather's mother reported her missing after two days. "She hasn't been home at all," said her mother, and Heather wasn't at our house either. The police talked to my stepsister for hours. My stepsister confessed that she and Heather had gone to a party; they'd lied, they were supposed to be at the movies—instead they put on high heels and wore mini-skirts and went to a party attended by college guys and drug users and older people.

My stepsister was grounded for six months, maybe even a year my parents threatened. "You slut, you tramp," my stepfather yelled at her, "I should have *known*—I should have *seen* it—you're both a couple of whores! Lying whores!"

Now this was on the news, too. The TV stations and papers called it "The Curse of Kitchen Creek Court." The people at the party were all questioned, but no one remembered Heather Gavin or had any idea what happened to her. Sometime during the party, my sister had lost track of Heather; she'd taken the drug Ecstasy and she had a few beers, someone she didn't know had given her a ride home.

Heather wrote in her diary:

I love XTC. I love the way it makes me feel. I love to fuck on it. I love to dance and laugh and listen to music on it. I wish I could take XTC every day, every hour, and the world would be very nice: there would be no fear and pain and tears and I would be happy all the time.

My stepsister made a break for emancipation. During her "imprisonment," as she called it, she discovered she was pregnant. Needless to say, my parents were *not* happy about this. My stepfather called her a slut some more and my mother said abortion was out of the question (we were Catholic), but the child could always be given up for adoption.

"I won't give my baby to strangers!" my stepsister screamed.

"You're fifteen!" my mother yelled back. "You're not ready to be a mother!"

My stepfather said, rather sarcastically, "I bet she doesn't even know who the father is."

"The father's name is William Dupris!" my stepsister claimed. "He loves me, he wants the baby, and he wants to marry me!"

"What is he," asked my stepfather, "some pimply stupid kid?"

"He's a *man*!"

"Hah!"

"Then let's meet him," said my mother, but that never happened. Three days later my sister escaped from the house and my parents filed a missing persons report. They said she, too, like Heather, could've been kidnapped. The police had no idea who William Dupris was and doubted he existed.

But he was real, apparently. Seven months later a letter arrived, with a photo of my sister and her newborn son, Wally. Wally had a big head and one drooping eye. My stepsister announced, in her letter, that she and William had been secretly married by a Reverend in the Church of the Almighty Universal Mind, they were living in Seattle, and her husband, a twenty-four-year-old bass player, was in a band that had just signed with V-2 Records in New York City.

Heather Gavin, meanwhile, showed up at the door to her mother's house a year later; all she wore was a tattered man's tank-top; she was ninety pounds and dirty, half-naked and mute. All that red hair had been shaved off her head and she had a black pentagram crudely tattooed on her scalp. She couldn't speak to the police, she refused to speak. No one had any idea what happened to her because she couldn't, or wouldn't, tell. She and her mother moved away from the neighborhood.

* * * * * * *

"She was held captive," Nancy said, "I can relate to that."

"You said you married her?" Sandra asked.

"I'm getting to that," I said.

* * * * * * *

I was nineteen and enrolled at Santa Monica College when I saw Heather Gavin again. This was at a party in West Hollywood. There were a lot of people at the party and when I spotted her; many memories came back. She'd put on weight, she was chubby, but her smile and laugh drew me to her. Her hair was curly now. I said: "I know you."

She looked at me and said: "I know you too. I think. Don't I?"

"Heather Gavin?"

"Holy fucking shit," she said, taking me by the arm and pressing me into a corner wall. "Look at you. You've grown up. You've become a man. Well," she said, flipping the hair out of her face, "I can talk now. I've been talking for seven years and it's good to speak."

"Are you doing well?"

"Forget *me*, what about your sister? Your parents?"

I told her: my stepsister was living in Idaho, on her third marriage and fifth child. My mother had passed away from cancer and my stepfather lived in Palm Springs now.

"So what about you," I said.

"Oh you know," she said, "this and that."

An hour later, she went home with me. I had a place in Venice; two roommates but I had my own room. She was twenty-six, the age difference wasn't that harsh, not like the summer days I was eleven and she was fifteen. I was very nervous and she thought this cute. I was not amused. I was afraid of doing the wrong thing.

"What's the matter?" Heather asked. "Don't you like me?"

"I've never done this before."

"What?"

"Sex," I said.

She didn't laugh at me like I thought she would. "It's okay," she said, but I didn't think it was: I was nineteen and the most I'd done with a girl was some heavy necking and a finger-bang. "It's okay, I know what to do," she said, and she undressed me, and she kissed me, and she made love to me, and she took my virginity.

I was in love; I had no idea how to tell Heather this. I was still afraid she would laugh. We spent a lot of time together the next two months; she worked as a "cocktail waitress" or so she claimed, but it wasn't until the day that I spilled my soul she told me the truth: she was a nude dancer at a "place" on Sunset Boulevard.

She didn't like meeting at my apartment; she had a studio in Korea Town and it was very cozy. And so I made the grand error of telling her my true feelings, and would she consider one day being my bride?

She stared at me like I was a suicide bomber and said, "Did I mislead you? Did I give you the wrong impression? If so, I am very sorry."

I said: "I thought—"

She said: "I like you, we have some really fucked-up history, you know, me and your sister and your family and that neighborhood and all, but don't get me wrong: this is getting laid. We're not, you know, boyfriend and girlfriend. I mean, you're not the only guy I sleep with. There are others."

I said: "I thought—"

"I popped your cherry," she said, rather coolly, "and that was a beautiful thing, and I thank you for letting me be the first woman. But I see now I made a mistake. It should've been that first time and *that time only*. I shouldn't have...well," she shrugged, and she smiled, and my heart felt ugly. "Do you even know what I *do?*" she said. "Do you know what I *am?*" she asked, and then she told me.

All I could do was nod.

She said: "I see now you know nothing about me."

This is when I blurted out my secret: that I had been in love with her since I was kid, that I had found and read her diary. "How can you say I don't know you? I *know* your very *soul.*"

"Oh my," she said, "you poor sweet thing. Your sister and me...we were *very bad* girls...we did *very bad* things."

I shook my head.

"And your stepfather...Jesus fucking Christ on a bloody cross, man."

"What?"

"One time, *one time only*, he fucked me."

I said: "I don't believe you!"

She stood. She went to closet. She brought her old diary, the one I had peeked at. "Your mother returned it,"

Heather said, "but she obviously didn't read it, and nor did you, not the whole thing." Heather looked through the thing, found a page near the end. "Didn't you see this?" she asked. "I guess not," she said. She gave me the diary, and I read:

> *I have made love to my best friend's father, it happened last night, and while I should feel shame and disgust, I really think it was the right thing to do at that time. I shall* not *let it happen again, but I've been aware of the way he's been looking at my body, which is okay: the lusty eyes all men have, and it seems it was bound to happen sooner or later and I know that*

I didn't read any further, I didn't witness the details. I handed her the diary and said: "No. Nothing like that ever happened. You used to make all kinds of things up; that's what my sister said."

"Do you even have an *idea* what happened to me when I vanished? Why I was unable to talk for a long time?" I shook my head, I didn't want to know, but she told me nonetheless: "I was drugged at that party, the party I went to with your dear sister, and the next thing I knew I was naked and chained in some kind of...I don't know, dungeon. I was held as a sex slave by this goddamn insane biker gang. They would play card games to determine which guy would screw me and how—which position, which hole in my body; and then the others would watch and cheer. They made me do awful things, they kept me drugged on meth and fed me little food. And one day they let me go. I've never even told my mother this, or anyone. You're the only person who knows."

* * * * * * *

"That's *it*?" Sandra said. "Oh, c'mon."

"We didn't talk for a couple of weeks," I said, "but she came back, she showed up at my door crying, she said she loved me, she said she missed me, she said she'd marry me. So we got married. It didn't last long. It wasn't good. She left me and I was all alone, again."

Silence.

"I'm scared," Sandra whispered in the dark.

"Soon it will all be over," Nancy said.

"We're not dead," I told her.

"Yet."

"Tell me a story," I said. "Keep your mind off death."

"Okay," said Nancy, "I'll tell you how I got into the sex trade."

CHAPTER TWENTY-SEVEN

"I wish I had good stories to entertain you," Sandra Boise said. "I don't. Nothing very interesting has ever happened to me. I eat, sleep and fuck. Sometimes I think I'm a machine, a fuck machine. Maybe you two want to hear about my ass. My first boyfriend was obsessed with it. He couldn't get his dick in there, he was so big and I was so small and never had anything in my ass. A friend told him I needed to be trained. He bought this 'anal training' kit online. I thought it was funny. He was serious. The kit came with a dozen assorted dildos and butt plugs, and plenty of Astroglide. We began with the butt plugs. Those were easy to get in. He had me walk around with a plug in my ass, even in public. I slept with one up there. I got used to it and even started to like it. Next was a small dildo. I got to like that. Over the next month, we worked our way up; he was patient and gradually got my little asshole to stretch, and I do mean stretch because by the end of the month, he was able to get some of this eight-inch, double-headed monster dildo in there, and it didn't hurt, it felt good and made me come. How's that for a story?"

CHAPTER TWENTY-EIGHT

Woke up to the sound of gunfire, men and women screaming, and more gun fire. I heard people running around, yelling out, shooting and being shot.

Then silence.

Then more gun fire.

Silence

More gun fire.

"What's going on?" Sandra asked.

The door opened. Several men walked down and turned the lights on. I saw the last man I ever expected to see in this situation: Tony, holding an Uzi in one hand and a nine-millimeter in the other. He was with two local Aruban men with guns.

"*There* you are," he said.

The men worked on releasing me and the girls.

I knew I was hallucinating—the lack of food, alcohol and sex will do that to a man.

"I'm real," Tony said.

"What the hell are you doing here?" I asked, sounding like Stephanie.

"I didn't hear back from you so I knew something went wrong," he said, sporting a big grin. "So what was I gonna do? Sit around going crazy? I came down here, hired me some local mercs, found the boat and raided the motherfucker. Lost a couple of guys, but we had the upper hand, they never expected us. We got this boat now."

"What about Hans?"

"Hans?"

"The guy who owns this."

"Dunno. He may be dead; he may be alive. Lot of nice women here. Where is Steph?"

"She should be here," I said.

Tony turned and was hugged by Nancy.

"My hero," she said.

"Damn, I love that! I come in and rescue the day! It's almost like I'm one of the *good guys.*"

* * * * * * *

Hans had gotten hit in the crossfire.

I looked at his dead body and spat on it.

Stephanie was found in one of the staterooms and she was just as flabbergasted by Tony's presence as I was. His coming in like this proved that he loved her. She vowed never to leave him again.

"You're gonna get a good beating when we get back home," he said.

"I deserve it," she said, like she had butterflies in her stomach.

We found some clothes for the three naked women and got the hell off the yacht and went back home.

CHAPTER TWENTY-NINE

Did it all lead to a happy ending?

Tony and Stephanie went back to their life at the club. Nancy followed, but she seemed to be thinking of another life. I could see it on her face: you spend a long period of time in captivity with a person, you learn to read them well.

Sandra Boise returned to L.A., but I heard she went up to San Francisco to be one of Mr. W's slaves.

Me, I returned to the Gaslamp Marina, happy as a fish in a new bowl of water to be back on my Catalina 30. It was good to be alone. It was good to drink alone. As far as I cared, I could never have another piece of ass as long as people stayed away from me with their problems, their desires, and their drama.

* * * * * * *

One night, I was drinking cheap beer and had a visitor.

Nancy. In a long overcoat.

"Hey, blue jay."

"Hi there."

"Can I come aboard, Captain?"

I bowed. "You may, madam."

She looked nice. She smelled nice. I realized that I missed the presence of women, and I could never go without having one every now and then.

"How goes it?" she asked.

"It goes."

"You look good."

"I look like shit."

"I think you look good," she said, and opened her coat, "do I?"

She was wearing nothing but shoes under that coat.

"Damn," I said, "you look great."

I got up, took the woman in my arms, and kissed her long and deep, as if we'd once been married, or in love.

"Will you fuck me?" she asked.

"Always," I said.

I took her into the cabin, laid her on my small bed, and slipped inside her and it was good. It was fantastic. It was exactly what I needed.

She needed it too.

It was quick, but I knew we had all night to screw.

"How goes it?" I asked her.

"Oh," she said, and laughed. "Stephanie ran away again."

"Is that why you're here? I'm not searching for that little crazymaker again. I don't care what Tony pays me."

"He's had it with her."

"He should."

"Why do men love women like that?"

I had to laugh. "You're asking me?"

She said: "So it was all for nothing, huh?"

"Isn't everything?" I said, feeling rather cynical.

We lay there for a while and then she asked, "So what do we do with our lives now?"

"We *fuck,*" I said.

And so we did, and it was very good like it should be. She got on top of me, the coat still on, her hothouse hole as wet as the Aruban beachfront in the middle of summer…and the bitch slowly rode up and down my throbbing peckerwood like the end of the universe was just around the corner.

About the Author

MICHAEL HEMMINGSON writes books in every possible genre he can: literary, western, SF, horror, noir, autobiography, erotica, narrative journalism, gonzo journalism, cultural anthropology, critical theory, critifiction, ethnography, sociology, and many other modes of academia including post-postmodern and post-colonial treatises. And private eye yarns. And film and TV studies. And smut. He also writes plays and screenplays. He has two independent feature films out: *The Watermelon* (LightSong Films) and *Stations* (Hemlene Entertainment). He has produced, directed, and written plays in San Diego and Los Angeles for the Fritz Theater and The Alien Stage Project. He lives in southern California, going back and forth from Hollywood to San Diego.

.